Saving Ukraine

Megan Hernandez, Volume 4

C. C. Chamberlane

Published by C. C. Chamberlane, 2022.

SAVING UKRAINE

First edition. March 26, 2022.

Copyright © 2022 C. C. Chamberlane.

ISBN: 978-1775373247

Written by C. C. Chamberlane.

SAVING UKRAINE
How Megan Hernandez, former Navy SEAL, saved Ukraine and prevented WW3

C.C.Chamberlane

Also by C. C. Chamberlane

Megan Hernandez
Samaela
The First Female Navy SEAL
Saving Ukraine

Standalone
Abbadon

Table of Contents

SAVING UKRAINE

C. C. CHAMBERLANE

Megan Hernandez had always excelled in school, on the field and in life. She was Einstein-smart and professional athlete talented. She was just the type organizations like the FBI and military identified early and watched closely to see if they had what it takes.

This book is about Megan after she left the teams. Being a Navy SEAL had defined her and now that training would help her help others.

Find out what motivated her to go down the road she did and what really makes her tick.

If you have comments or ideas, please email us directly at CCChamberlane@gmail.com

@ccchamberlane

ISBN Print – 978-1-7753732-4-7
Copyright 2022 C.C.Chamberlane
Published by C.C.Chamberlane

This is a work of fiction but contains actual facts in order to provide perspective on the events.

Thank you for respecting the hard work of this author.

If you have feedback, comments or ideas for stories please contact me at CCChamberlane@gmail.com

Acknowledgements

This book is dedicated to the brave women who serve in the various branches of the military. They had to work tirelessly to earn the right to fight and now that they have, they will never relinquish that power.

After a rousing response to ABBADON, C.C.Chamberlane's first book, I am pleased to offer another novel about Megan Hernandez for your reading pleasure. This book is dedicated to all the loyal fans who have read ABBADON, SAMAELA, and The First Female Navy SEAL and I hope you like this one just as much. Thank you all for your support.

About the Author – C.C. Chamberlane

This is the fourth fact-influenced-fiction crime novel in a series that features the exploits of Megan Hernandez.

I have always been a true crime type person as these stories are multi-layered and enjoyable to read. I have always been a fan of the genre. Studying troubled and unique minds is especially interesting.

Keep an eye on our Facebook page at C.C.Chamberlane and watch for the next title in the series.

Prologue

As all parents tend to be, both Esai and I are immensely proud of all our children. All have had success in their lives but our only daughter, Megan, came closest to following in our footsteps.

As the first female navy SEAL, the world found out just how special she was. The teams quickly became her life. While she really could not discuss much with us, we knew the danger she was in on each and every mission. We also knew, as both of us were in high level law enforcement, that there was likely nobody better equipped to handle that danger than "our little girl."

It seems odd to call a woman who can easily defeat multiple attackers, kills people for a living and defends her country without question "our little girl" but it was the truth. Of course, it had also become a bit of a joke amongst us, with her brothers ribbing Megan mercilessly about it. She takes it all in stride and always plays along which is one of her more endearing qualities.

I think her brothers weren't overly tough on her partly due to the fact that at some point they had become aware she could easily defeat them one at a time or all at once. She truly is an amazing woman.

Now, after 12 years as a SEAL and having successfully completed more missions than we know about, she was retiring.

Due to the danger, they are in, and the physical challenges of doing what they do a Navy SEAL's full hitch is only twelve years.

At any time after that they have the option of being moved to a different branch of the Navy or retiring with full pay.

As much as Megan relished being a SEAL and accepted willingly all the challenges and ever-present danger of her calling, she was ready to leave. She had always felt that there was more she could do. Something else that would allow her to utilize her crazy skills and still help the world. At this point she was unsure what and planned to take the year to relax and regenerate but still remain in fighting form.

To Megan, training, sparring, and fighting were natural ways for her to relax. She often said training allowed her to think, to focus her thoughts on things SHE wanted to do for a change and not simply what the Navy demanded her to do.

She would find her next calling quite unexpectedly thanks to a long-time girlfriend of hers.

Chapter 1 – How It All Started

It was the end of summer and I had had a great few months since leaving my SEAL brothers. We still got together from time to time but it was different. They were still active, and I was not. The dynamic between us all had clearly changed. We did not see each other as often and the wives and girlfriends seemed to act differently around me. I suppose we just drifted apart. It was a complicated process for me after sharing so many life-threatening situations together.

I had a few girlfriends now who knew I had been in the military but had no idea I was a SEAL. I preferred to keep it like that, it was clean and easy. I was usually the stable one in any group of females. I think facing your own mortality regularly and experiencing close up life and death on an almost daily basis calms you. At least it can calm you when you're done.

SEALs receive ongoing, extensive training not only physically, but psychologically as well. You are trained to learn to accept almost anything, deal with it and then put it behind you. Not everyone can do this as the thousands of cases of severe PTSD in our military will prove, but the training is there. I was one of those who was able to adapt, who fully accepted everything we were offered. That acceptance and willingness to learn meant that, for what I had done and things I had seen, I was relatively well adjusted.

That did not mean that I was 100% fine by any stretch of the imagination. Every now and then something would happen and the SEAL in me would just show up.

I had no inkling that today would be one of those days.

Chapter 2 - Becky's Ex

I was having a nice lunch with my friend Becky. We were sitting on a patio enjoying the sun, a couple of cocktails, and some tasty Mexican food. Becky had been single for almost three years now and shared her child with her ex-husband who had always been a bit of a wild card. I had met him a few times when they were still married and wasn't really a fan, but it wasn't for me to say.

Of course, once they were broken up and there was no chance of them getting back together, I felt free to share my true thoughts.

He liked to make a deal out of me being a SEAL and even claimed that I got special treatment because I was female. I used to laugh and point out that the only special treatment I got was everything was made a little more difficult for me. He often said he would like to go a round or two with me as there was no way I could defeat him.

I remember thinking that, as a SEAL, if I were to get into a scrap with him, I would be the one in trouble. Not because he would likely even lay a hand on me but because I could easily take him down. One of the key things I have learned is that when you are highly trained in fighting skills you are the one who eats the assault charge, no matter how it started.

Becky was telling me how he was trying to be pushier about their custody agreement and she was scared. His name was Abdul-Fattah (which means servant of God the conqueror). He spoke Dari, more commonly referred to as Farsi, which is a dialect of the Persian language.

When they were together, I tried to be accepting of him even though he could have just been another Afghan rebel to me. I did see what she saw in him and how they ended up married. Although, he was a tall, olive-skinned, dark-haired guy who could best be described as swarthy.

I remember when they were dating, and things started to get serious he seemed like a great guy. Soon after they were married the Persian/ Afghan in him came out. He seemed to treat Becky as a chattel, his property. I didn't like the way he spoke to her often, but they already had a child so there was little that could be done.

That was up until he threatened her, and she was able to record it on her smart phone. She used that recording to first secure an order of protection for her and her child and then get a divorce. They had been divorced now for three years and their daughter was just turning four. He had only seen her intermittently since the divorce.

At first the supervised visits went smoothly and then their daughter shared that she and her dad had talked about Afghanistan and going there. Becky just lost it and went through all kinds of machinations in an attempt to revoke visitation but was unsuccessful. Her daughter had a backpack that she always carried with her, and Becky had a tracking chip sewn into the lining, just in case. She could track that chip via her cellphone anywhere in the world thanks to the internet. It gave her some semblance of confidence that he could never take her away, at least not permanently.

We were talking through all kinds of things when Abdul suddenly appeared at our table.

Chapter 3 - Who's Tougher Now?

He stood smiling down at us smugly. He bent closer to our table, looked at Becky and said, "You cannot, you will not, keep our daughter from me." She mentioned the order of protection and said he couldn't be here, that she would call the police. He spat at her, so I grabbed his arm only to move him away.

"Keep your hands off me bitch," he scowled. I told him to leave quietly right now and nothing more would happen. He started to twist my arm and said he would leave when he was good and ready, and I should keep my comments to myself. He twisted as far as I was willing to let him, so I stood quickly and got behind him.

In two seconds, he was on the ground begging me to let him go as I employed a hand-based restraint using his thumb. It was very painful and, unless you were very well trained, difficult to break. Unless, of course, you chose to break your own thumb. I told him to stay calm and I would let him get to his feet. He said something in Farsi as I let him stand and he walked away.

The rest of our lunch went well, and Becky was calm by the time it was over. We each went to our cars and, my spidey senses were tingling, so I decided to follow her home.

She drove calmly through the neighborhood, and I stayed a few cars behind. I parked up the street and wasn't at all surprised when, as she exited her car in the garage, I saw Abdul scoot through the door before it closed.

I parked my car and walked toward their house. I knew there was no way he would hurt her or kill her, but I still knew I should be there for her. I could call the police, but they would take forever and likely not do anything anyway. The law did nowhere near enough to protect vulnerable women. I knew I could, being the least vulnerable woman I know.

I quietly walked around their house and was able to peak in the kitchen window. I saw Abdul standing over Becky as she sat in a chair. He looked menacing and upset and he was yelling things I couldn't hear. I wasn't about to wait so I went to the back door and walked in.

"What are you doing here, this is none of your business infidel." I just smiled and told him to calm down, neither one of us needed any trouble. He came toward me, and I pleaded with him to stop. "Please Ab, don't do this."

He got closer and was loading up to take a swing at me. I let him launch the punch, which I easily side stepped and then used his own arm to put him into a choke hold. I let him down to the floor before he was completely out, and the idiot sat there briefly but then came up swinging. I was done with the Mr. Nice Guy routine when his punch almost connected.

I drove a straight fist directly into his solar plexus completely knocking the wind out of him. He attempted two more swings and I decided I was finished with this charade. My next blow landed squarely on his jaw, and he went down in a heap, out cold. When he returned to consciousness, I was sitting in a chair across from him.

"Look Abdul, I am willing to let you go but if you attack me or Becky again, I guarantee you will have broken bones." I went on to explain it was his decision what to do but our next call was to the police. He stood and left and that was that.

I was able to find out from a friend of mind in Homeland Security that he had returned to Afghanistan. He had lived in Balkh which is considered one of the oldest cities in the world. It was named the Mother of Cities by the Arabs. There are ancient ruins everywhere and monuments that include the Nine Dome Mosque and the Green Mosque

During my time as a SEAL, I had actually seen Balkh while on a secret mission. (Weren't they ALL secret?) I saw the Nine Domes Mosque and was impressed that something more than 1,000 years old and only 20 metres square was still standing. It is one of the best-preserved Islamic buildings and, while not mecca, many still travel to see it.

It was sometimes hard for me to reconcile how some of these people could come from such a beautiful place. There were places like this all over Afghanistan and it always amazed me how they were spared from rockets, bombs, and all manner of attack.

The good news was that Abdul was back there, hopefully to stay. Becky hadn't seen him in two years and my friend at Homeland had not advised of him showing up on their radar. Things were seeming quite smooth for the moment.

Chapter 4 – Where Is Allyssa?

Everything seemed fine until I received a frantic call from Becky. She asked if Alyssa had come to my house and said she couldn't find her. I said she wasn't and then went straight to her house. Becky was beside herself saying she was sure Abdul had taken her. I begged her not to jump to conclusions, but I immediately put a call in to my friend Alexis at DHS.

In the current geopolitical climate, there was no more powerful or influential branch than the Department of Homeland Security. They could get away with almost anything. The FBI was limited to US citizens and our own soil. The CIA was everything outside the US, but DHS had carte blanche to do whatever they wished, wherever they wanted. There was no better place to have a contact than there. I have known Alexis for years too and consider her one of my closest friends.

Unfortunately, she was on vacation and not returning until the following day. I explained that to Becky while we put in a missing child report, and they created an amber alert. I knew we wouldn't hear anything right away, so I stayed with Becky to try and keep her calm. The next morning, I called Alexis first thing.

She checked and apologized as she told me Adbul had been in and out of the country.

He had left only hours earlier from a private jet at John Wayne airport. Dammit! I couldn't believe this had happened. Becky was immediately on the phone to anyone who would speak to her.

Becky had activated the tracking chip and we were glad that Alyssa obviously was still in possession of her backpack. I explained we had no extradition treaty with Afghanistan so there was nothing the law could do for her. She could try to plead with Abdul but we both agreed that would achieve nothing. She asked if I knew of anyone, could I get someone to help.

That moment was when I knew what I must do. I looked at her and said I could try but it would be outside the law. I went on to explain there was no guarantee that I could leave Abdul alive if I was able to get her back. She put her hand on mine and said simply, "Do whatever you can to get Alyssa back to me, please."

I said I would and started making some calls. Getting in and out of Afghanistan would be no small feat. Actually, I felt confident I could get in easy enough. With my skin tone I could certainly pass for a local. Getting back out, with a child who was not mine, would be far more difficult. I finished my calls and sat Becky down.

I explained that there were many hurdles to overcome, and certainly no guarantees, but I was willing to do whatever I could.

I explained to her the situation about exiting Afghanistan and the challenges. That was when she shared something I had never known. Apparently, she had inherited a pile of money. Most of it was invested and it was all well hidden, mostly in the Cayman Islands. That was how she kept it secret from Abdul. The Caymans are this generation's "Swiss bank account."

She went on to tell me that the advantage of holding her cash there and the fact it was untraceable meant she could do whatever she wanted. It also meant that she had access to numerous people available in that neck of the woods who were willing to do things for money. Usually lots of money, but money was really no object here.

I told Becky that all I would need would be a private jet waiting for me at the Mazar-i-Sharif international airport. It was a mere 24 kilometres from Balkh and regularly had private jets flying in and out. The biggest challenge was that from that airport to LA was slightly more than 12,000 km as the crow flies.

I knew, from my previous life, that one of the executive jets that could do this (I believe the only one) was the Gulfstream G650ER. It is the extended range version of the G650, and it has a range of 14,000 km. It also flies at 85% of the speed of sound which is over 1,000 km per hour. That means Balkh to LA could be as quick as 14 hours. Flying at 35,000 feet is also a bonus as that is typically commercial airspace.

I explained to Becky that if she was going to "ask around" she should do so only though a trusted and well-known contact, if she had one, based in the Caymans. She advised that her bank provided a concierge-type service through an individual and he was as trusted as the bank itself. She knew of people who had this fellow arrange things and all spoke very highly of him.

I left her with a list of things to lay out including the fact the flight manifest would be showing one person less than who was actually flying.

We also had to ensure that access to the aircraft at the Mazar-i-Sharif airport was easy and private. I told her it might be a clever idea to find out if this guy can also provide two bodyguards in case help was needed at the airport.

I went home to sit down and plan as much as I could. Fortunately, with Balkh being such a high tourist area I might be able to stay under the radar. I would only find that out when I began planning. I toyed with the idea of talking to Alexis at DHS but decided that was too dangerous.

The US wasn't going to risk an international incident to get back one child. The politicians talk a big game but when the rubber hits the road those cake-eaters all disappear.

The good thing was Balkh was in a region I was familiar with and within easy driving distance of some major spots. It was South of the border to Uzbekistan although I had NO intention of going there. The whole region was one gang of warlords or crooks after another, and the Russian mob was nothing to sneeze at either. If I did get into trouble, I could exit via India but that would be the best of a bunch of bad choices. A plane direct to LA was the best option.

I had an idea roughed out and was continuing to dig up intel, but I would have to wait until Becky let me know she had the plane arranged. I would deliver half the cash when the plane left the ground, and the other half would be wire-transferred when we were safely on the ground in Los Angeles.

Chapter 5 – Like I Had Never Left The SEALS

It was like a mission when I was on the teams. Planning, planning and more planning. The way to stay alive was to plan for every contingency and triple check every detail. It was also critical to have more than one back up plan just in case. You never knew what might happen or how things could change.

I suppose if worst came to worst, I could always get myself to Bagram or Kandahar, each held a US base. That would be only a last ditch and worst-case scenario, however. I would need to gather as much information as I could, and once Becky arranged the plane I would leave for Afghanistan. When I get her daughter safely in hand, I will let her know via sat phone to get the plane in position.

I never thought I would ever return to this place. I had seen a great deal of pain and inflicted my share of it too. Fortunately, I still had some Afghan contacts there who could move me around in vehicles safely. They had bulletproof hidden compartments and virtually free reign of the areas where I would be. They wanted to keep the US on their side. American money is as good as gold around the world and, to be honest, we also turned a blind eye to their lucrative drug trade.

I gathered up all the maps I required and purchased a sat phone along with anything else I needed that I could travel with. Fortunately, my contacts on the ground in Afghanistan could hook me up with some weapons.

I wasn't quite sure how I would get into the country at this point, but I had a few ideas. It was time to reconnect with a few of my SEAL brothers and talk turkey.

I met up with my two best buds from my unit, Sonny, and Travis. Both were your textbook Navy SEALs, but both also were willing to color outside the lines a bit. Travis was a master-chief (they are the leaders of a team) so he had some stroke, and I was really hoping we could come to an agreement. IF they could take me somewhere it would be on super short notice.

When a team spins up (leaves for a mission) they typically get little notice. On the order of two to three hours was not out of the ordinary. I would need to be fully prepared and completely packed. If I were able to hitch a ride on one of their flights, I would be able to bring some of my own weapons so I had a separate bag I could add to my stash. A garotte, a couple of Berettas and ammo and a ka-bar knife.

Not my actual SEAL knife but one exactly like it. There was nothing better in close quarters than a ka-bar as you could easily shred someone's heart in a second.

It provided me great comfort to have it strapped to my body somewhere. I packed and repacked and was now content that I had everything ready.

I met up with Sonny and Travis at a bar where we had never been as our usual haunts were filled with other forces people. We all high fived and hugged it out and then sat down over a round of Dos Equis. I explained to them my situation and what I had to do.

I told them not to feel obligated but wondered if there was any way they could get me to Kandahar or Bagram so I could make my way to Balkh? They both whistled and said that was a tall order and could even jeopardize their careers. Travis asked the reason and once I explained it to him, he said he would find a way. We had a couple of beers and then went our separate ways with Travis telling me he would be in touch.

Now that I knew they were on board I went back to Alexis at DHS. I knew they used contractors all over the world to get information and get things done that could not ever lead back to them. I explained to her that I had the cooperation of my SEAL buds and asked if there was any way she could arrange for me to have passage to Afghanistan under the auspices of Homeland Security.

She said there actually were a few things going on and she would let me know. Luckily, she got back to me before Travis or Sonny did and let me know she had a small contract in the area. She could requisition me for that and that would explain away my presence on a US air force plane. The Navy did not transport SEALS themselves as they had no aircraft other than fighters and carrier-based planes. The SEALS always hitched rides with the air force or army so this was nothing new.

So, everything was set up. I just needed to have some patience and wait for Sonny to get back in touch. It would be too dangerous for Travis to contact me as team leaders are under some pretty severe scrutiny. Not that everyone else isn't! Some dove in the government is always looking to hang us out to dry for bending rules!

It took a couple of weeks, but my phone rang early on a Friday morning. The boys were being spun up and I had exactly three hours to get to the plane. I was really happy I wasn't flying commercial as being able to bring a few of my own weapons would make life a lot easier.

The DHS advantage was also that when we landed, I would have a local contact and vehicle, which was a huge bonus. I got on the plane fine with most of the guys appearing glad to see me. It looked like Travis had already told them I would be here as none seemed surprised at all.

I strapped into my seat, put on my headphones, and hoped to drift off for at least part of the 28-hour flight.

Chapter 6 – Meeting Alexis

As the aircraft rumbled along, I got to thinking about Alexis and how we met. Alexis has really come through for me on this and I was impressed. We met through our mutual friend Norie. As a powerful Assistant District Attorney for Los Angeles, Norie interacted with many people from many agencies. The Department of Homeland Security was just one of them. As she mentioned to me, she had met Alexis a few times and figured we could all be friends.

Norie ended up bringing her along to one of Kathy and Jonathon's parties and that was where we were first introduced. Norie was bang on in her assessment. Alexis and I hit it off as if we had been friends our whole lives. It felt a bit odd to me at first as I had never had that happen. Mostly I am a little more cautious and always wary of someone who seems to be too good a fit right off the bat. After all, that was exactly how I embedded myself in a dangerous drug cartel.

There were no worries here though, Alexis was authentic. She looked at the world as Norie and I did in a lot of ways. I suppose the main difference between Norie, and Alexis was DHS did not seem encumbered or limited by the law. The Department of Homeland Security could do, and get away with, just about anything they wanted it seemed. I was certain this would help me in both the near and long term.

The power of DHS seemed limitless. As a former SEAL, I knew we could get away with a lot of things.

Mostly everything we did, however, was sanctioned by our leaders and the politicians around them. There were a minimal number of instances where we came close to bending the rules of engagement, but few ever did. DHS appeared to have carte blanche when it came to activities surrounding the protection of our nation. Or at least, what THEY said was the protection of our nation.

I was aware there were dark sites and places like Gitmo where suspects could be hidden for days, weeks, even years until they gave up accurate intel. I was certain that some simply disappeared. This was not my situation though.

When I first explained to Alexis that I needed her help she immediately asked why. I felt comfortable telling her the whole truth. When I explained that Becky's ex-husband had kidnapped their daughter and I was going to bring her back she was on board right away. Apparently, she had a friend who had been in the same situation, and he still had her. Even with all the power she had at DHS there was nothing she could do. I filed that one away for future discussions.

We got together once more before I asked for her help directly to get me on a plane and into Afghanistan. I was surprised she was able to get it done but I would soon learn that I shouldn't have been surprised at all!

Chapter 7 – Back in Afghanistan

I faded in and out until the noise of the landing gear deploying woke me up with a start. It felt odd to be landing back at Bagram Air Base with SEALs but me not be a part of that team.

Bagram Air Base is in the Parwan province of Afghanistan and houses US Army, Navy, Marines and even Coast Guard. Covering all the bases I assumed. There was also a civilian staffed group that was the US platform for the east. The Parwan detention facility is located close-by and there is a little-known "Black jail" cordoned off within the base.

This Black jail is run by the Defense Intelligence agency and the Special Operations Forces. Windowless cells with a single 24-hour light bulb always on is a place you never want to find yourself. There were rumours of beatings, sleep deprivation and putting prisoners into stress positions in attempts to extract knowledge. I had little doubt that DHS had access to this place as well.

Bagram was not terribly far away from the Mazer-i-Sharif airport I would be departing from if everything goes according to plan. Balkh, where I was headed, was just shy of 399 kilometres from Bagram Air Base.

You typically got there using the A-76 road, but my route would need to be more circuitous. I knew it would take at least ten hours or more to complete the journey.

Alexis had arranged for me to have a room in the on-camp dorms for which I was thankful. It would give me time to rest up and re-confirm my plans. I originally thought I would be making most of the journey on my own, but I would find out the next day that Alexis had made other arrangements. As I walked from the aircraft to the dorm area a few of my SEAL team buddies walked with me. We were all going to be in the same general area, and it felt good to know that.

I may not be an active SEAL any longer but there was no doubt they would have my back if required. The bond was for life. It always had been and always would be. When you fight shoulder to shoulder knowing that no matter what happens, they will get you home or you will get them home it is a powerful connection. The Trident may connect you outwardly, and visibly to the world, but it was your hearts and souls that were inseparably linked.

I sat around outside with the boys for a couple of hours and then excused myself to my room. I had to make contact with my in-country connection that Alexis had setup.

I got through using a secure line and Aziz said he would arrive no later than 6:00 AM and we would need to get rolling quickly.

He explained he had a specially outfitted vehicle with a hidden bulletproof compartment designed to carry two adults. He was a farmer who hated what the Taliban and others were doing to his country and been working with America for years. Once I got the full story, I was surprised that he had lasted so long doing what he was doing. Clearly, he was exceptionally good at it.

Chapter 8 – On The Road To Balkh

Luckily, for the first few hours there were no danger zones that would require me to be stashed away. I was thankful as it gave me time to get comfortable with Aziz and learn more about him. Turned out his wife and children has been murdered while he was working out in his wheat fields.

He heard and saw nothing as he had a large amount of land that he farmed. Backing up against the mountains, it was one of the few areas that received enough moisture to support farming. Only about 6% of the land is Afghanistan is being farmed so he was an important cog in their food chain. He believed that was why he was targeted.

He was never able to confirm what exactly happened but when he returned from the fields he was met with bloodshed in and around his barn. They even shot the two goats he relied on for milk. He was devasted and vowed at that moment to do everything in his power to avenge his family's murder. He had been doing so ever since.

I was then quite comfortable telling him more about what I was doing. He was familiar with Balkh and the surrounding areas. His brother-in-law even lived there and when he found out about what had happened to Aziz's wife, his sister, and his nieces and nephews he too was livid. They did not usually work together. Each mounted their own resistance in their own way.

Fortunately, this was not one of those times. His brother-in-law had offered us a place to hide while we were in the region.

We stopped at what felt like about halfway there and Aziz suggested I get into my hiding spot. I chuckled and said it was highly unlikely that whomever we ran into our here would be able to overpower me, but he said that wasn't the point. He was able to operate as he had been by moving through the region as normally as possible. Trips to deliver or pick up farming items, deliver crops, purchase fertilizer etc etc. In this way he was able to move freely about thanks to no suspicious activity and no deaths that might attract scrutiny.

As he was explaining the words I thought, "of course," and realized I perhaps was not SEAL sharp at that moment. I would ensure that did not happen again and would get back to training my mind as religiously as I trained my body. Mistakes here got you killed.

I grabbed all traces as we pulled over and I climbed into the container that appeared like a fuel tank. It was actually a large fuel tank that was very shallow. The bottom two thirds held the secret compartment. He closed the hatch once I was inside, and I settled in. It was confined but not completely uncomfortable.

He suggested I may have to remain in the there until we got to his brother's compound just outside Balkh. The thought of more than four hours in here wasn't pleasant but it was the safest option.

I knew that once I was moving around Balkh dressed in traditional Afghan clothing with my darker colored skin I would fit in well. On the open road however, it was simply too dangerous. I had clothes that were waiting for me at Bagram when I arrived.

Traditional Afghan dress usually included solid colour trousers and long shirt with long sleeves and a belt, or the solid colour trousers, a long-sleeved dress over that and sometimes a waistcoat. There was also the Burqa or Niqab that either covered the whole head and face as a veil does or the more familiar hijab which covers the hair and neck. In rural Afghanistan, the complete covering was more typical but urban areas like Kabul, Balkh and others saw more open faces.

It was warm to be sure but the safety it afforded me would have made any temperature tolerable. While I could not move effortlessly around the area it would be much easier. Balkh was only about a dozen kilometres North of Mazar-i-Sharif and 74 kilometres South of the border with Uzbekistan.

Balkh itself was an interesting city, one of the oldest in the world and situated on the Silk Road routes that ran between east and west. Balkh was originally the head of the government, until Genghis Kahn and the Mongols destroyed the city in 1220. It is a unique area in Afghanistan.

In ancient times the region was known as Bactria. The Balkab river created an area very suitable for irrigation and growing crops that included grapes, sugar cane and oranges. As you may have guessed, it is also the home of the Bactrian Camel. The Cadillac of Camels if you ask an Afghan.

I went over all of the history of the area to calm my mind and help time pass more quickly for me during this confinement. I also knew that, thanks to its proximity to a number of borders, there were a few languages spoken there.

Dari and Pashto languages were of course prominent, but you also heard a lot of Uzbek and Turkmen. I wasn't planning to strike up any conversations, but it was good to know that my knowledge of Uzbek may come in handy. As a Turkic language, there are many similar in the area, so I knew I could count on that if it was required.

After what seem like a full day, but was actually less than four hours, I felt us stopping briefly and then pulling ahead.

I heard what sounded like a large door close and then Aziz opened the compartment. I was relieved to get out and stretch and Aziz introduced me to his brother-in-law. He said there would be no names used as it would be safer in case anything happened to any one of us. I got that and simply smiled and nodded.

We spent the evening eating local foods in his brother-in-law's modest home. It was basic but hearty food. He explained how he was mere miles away from the ancient Nine Dome Mosque and the significance of that structure. It is said the mosque was most likely constructed around the year 794! It was amazing the ruins were as well preserved as they were, but I supposed that was the benefit of such an arid climate.

I knew where I needed to be the next day and Aziz was going to help me get there. I had a recording of the girl's mother with me so I could play it for Alyssa, and she would know I am a friend here to rescue her.

Chapter 9 – A Daring Rescue

At first Becky thought naming their daughter after a mythical Persian Princess was unique and adorable. Her given name was Kashm, but she was most often referred to as Kash or Princess. We had agreed that when I first met her, I would call her Princess as that had always been her mother's pet name for her. Prior to the kidnapping, Becky had legally changed Kashm's first name to Alyssa. She wanted as few lingering memories of Abdul-Fattah that she could.

I agonized over my next steps in the plan. I knew that Becky did not really want Abdul dead, but I also knew how men from this area typically acted and thought. Even if I were to escape safely and return Alyssa to her mother the threat of Abdul returning would always be looming over her head. I already knew that I would eliminate him once his daughter was safely in my custody and anxious to get back to her mother. I just had to ensure she had no knowledge of what I was going to do. I truly hoped Abdul would be stupid enough to force my hand as that would make it easier for me.

I knew that the next day Abdul would be at services as he was a devout Sunni. Although Balkh had been a center of Buddhism it had long been taken over by Islam, the bulk being Sunni.

I found it an odd juxtaposition that one could be "religious" and yet hate others, disrespect and abuse women and even steal a child. Sure, it was his daughter, but I knew what life there would likely bring her and it was not a pretty picture.

I slept soundly that night knowing that I had a plan in place with every contingency I could think of accounted for. That still did not mean it was a done deal nor did it mean I would relax until we were both on that jet back to LA.

Aziz stayed at home while his brother-in-law drove me in the truck in which we had travelled to Balkh. Night was falling and the evening services would have just gotten under way. I felt that the best approach would be to take Alyssa and get her safely back to the truck while I wanted for Abdul. I realized that might compromise our safety so I decided I would enter his house when he returned.

I knew if there were other women there that they were likely already being mistreated so might be sympathetic. There was chance they wouldn't be though, so I decided to get into the house and subdue whoever was there. I had some powerful tranquilizers with me and would use them to set the stage for when Abdul returned.

We parked close to the house, and I moved quietly through the dirt street. I posted the house and watched for about fifteen minutes using my compact night vision binoculars to confirm occupants. Thankfully, I only saw two along with Alyssa. This part would be easy. I gained entry and subdued the two women once Alyssa was in bed.

I went to her room and showed her the video from her mother. As I took my hand off her mouth, she didn't make a sound and just hugged me.

I told her to wait her under the covers and not to move no matter what she heard. I explained we would be leaving tonight to see her mommy. I left the phone with her as she wanted to watch the video message over and over. Just as I hit play, I heard the front door open. I had no idea who it was as services could not be over yet.

I peaked around the corner and was relieved to see Abdul, and only Abdul. I stepped into the light and startled him, and he began to ask what I was doing there and then tried to run towards Alyssa's room. I stopped him in his tracks, and he began swinging wildly at me. I really didn't feel like playing around here so I delivered a round house kick that landed right on his jaw. He went down like he had been shot.

I didn't need to restrain him at all, so I just sat there across from him waiting for him to wake up. I needed to give him a chance. A chance to leave Becky and her daughter alone, a chance for him to stay alive.

I did not really WANT to kill him but if I had to I certainly would. As soon as his eyes opened, he came at me.

I captured his arm as he tried to punch and subdued him, taking him to the floor. He was easy for me to hold with one arm as I didn't want him out cold. I begged him to simply let us leave and stay out of their lives forever. He scowled as he said NEVER and started to struggle. I asked him one more time truly hoping he would agree but he kept it up. I reached down to my leg and unstrapped my ka-bar. I used my free arm to reach around and drive the knife into his heart, the serrated part of the blade tearing it apart easily. He was gone in seconds.

I cleaned up a little, gave the two women an additional tranquilizer shot that would keep them out for hours and moved Abdul to the other room. I threw a carpet over the blood on the floor and got Alyssa and a few of her things and we returned to the truck. It was dangerous to be out here at night and I had no idea if Alyssa would be quiet so we both got into the secret compartment.

In minutes we were back at the house and Aziz was greeting us. I contacted Becky and said we were ready to go. She needed to get that G650ER to Mazar-i-Sharif as soon as possible. She said she had been ready for two days and the aircraft was staged in New Delhi.

It was 1,301 kilometers to Mazar-e-Sharif from there so the G650 could do it in a little more than an hour. It would take time to ensure the flight was registered and the back story was solid.

We waited as Alyssa watched the video over and over again, now extremely excited to see her mother. She said she was anxious to get home as soon as possible so I explained we would be going as fast as we could. We needed to arrive at the airport only minutes before the jet landed. There would be a Saudi prince disembarking when it landed so that would require isolation and that was how we would get on the plane. There had to be a rock-solid cover story as in this neck of the world they would have no qualms about shooting down a civilian aircraft.

We got all our things ready, and I dressed Alyssa in some warm clothes and did my best to hide her face, just in case we were spotted anywhere.

I remembered the Mazar airport, and I thought the International Airport moniker was really a bit much.

It looked like a tiny, small-town airport somewhere in rural America. The good thing was that, even with the military presence and security, it would not be too difficult to get us onto the aircraft. We parked in a field hidden by trees as close to the runway as we could get.

I had worked with Alexis at Homeland Security to get a us a free pass through security. That was about as much as she could be involved.

I sure would have preferred rolling into Bagram Air Base and getting back on a C-140 or something similar but that simply could not happen. It would be a military and diplomatic nightmare if we were discovered.

We watched and waited patiently and then I saw it. Even in the darkness it looked sleek and beautiful. The tail lit up to proudly display the G650ER name. The eight side windows glowing like portholes on a ship, two powerful jets bringing it smoothly to the ground. We moved quickly over to the fence where a guard let us in and we got into his vehicle, crouching down so as not to be seen.

The pilot had to park back from the terminal as he needed to top off his fuel to ensure, even if we had to detour or ran into weather, that we could make it to LA. He did so and as the engines wound down, we watched as the door opened and the steps went to the ground.

A princely-looking fellow descended down the stairs. Once he was out of sight, Alyssa and I immediately scurried back up.

We exchanged the cramped space in the vehicle we were in for some much more comfortable accommodations.

Once we were fueled up, they pulled up the steps and closed the door and we immediately started taxiing toward the runway. In less than a minute since we had boarded, we were now easing smoothly into the night sky.

I couldn't help but think "so, this is how the rich people live." We were surrounded by thick leather seats and sofas and there was even a bedroom in the rear of the aircraft. There was a pilot and a co-pilot and once we were on our way the co-pilot came back and said it was nice to have us aboard. He extended his hand and shook mine saying, "it's an honor to have you aboard ma'am, thank you for your service." I smiled up at him and said simply, "Thank you for yours too."

I got Alyssa to sleep in the bedroom and I returned to the seats. I reclined in hopes of watching the world whiz by at over 1,000 kilometres per hour but must have passed completely out. That often happened to me after a mission. The boys used to get so pissed at me, claiming I could sleep anywhere. I drifted off feeling tremendously satisfied.

When I awoke, it was bright in the cabin and the co-pilot was lightly tapping me on the shoulder telling me we were a half hour out. I was shocked. I couldn't believe I had been out virtually the whole trip.

He told me not to worry, Alyssa was up with them. She was very inquisitive and not a bother at all he said.

Chapter 10 – Reunited

I stayed in my seat and watched as we glided quietly over Los Angeles. We were landing at John Wayne airport, which is in orange county, rather than LAX. In any other city but LA, John Wayne would be a sizeable international airport. In Los Angeles it was simply a different place to fly in and out of. The stars and rich folk liked it because it was easy to get to and better located than LAX.

It was also a little easier to fly under the radar. I heard the landing gear deploy with the accompanying whoosh of air as we approached the runway. I barely felt us touch down as the pilot eased the aircraft back to earth. I could hear Alyssa up front, still asking questions as we taxied toward the hangar.

We pulled directly inside the hangar and once the engines were shut down the massive doors began to close behind us. The pilot came back and said he was glad they could be of help and then we grabbed our bags and waited as the co-pilot opened the large door and the stairs automatically deployed.

Becky was standing there, along with my friend Alexis and I had to hold Alyssa back, so she didn't run and fall. As we stepped onto the hangar floor Becky came running over, scooped up Alyssa and held her tight.

They were both ecstatic. Becky caught my eye with an inquisitive look, and I just nodded my head yes, assuming she would know what that meant.

Becky hugged me and thanked me profusely and then I walked away to a car with Alexis. We sat in the back seat, and I thanked her for everything she had done to accomplish this. She just laughed and said the whole thing would have been nothing without me or, worse yet, could have caused an international incident. Before dropping me off at my house Alex mentioned that I should rest for a while but added that she had been speaking with Norie.

She said that the three of us really needed to get together for lunch once I was wound down. I chuckled as I said, "Alex, that was a piece of cake. Sometimes I think you forget what I used to do for a living." She smiled back at me replying, "It wasn't that I forgot what you did. It was more that it still amazes me that you were an honest-to-God Navy SEAL.

Chapter Eleven – A New Calling

As I sat on my balcony looking out over the ocean it came to me that I had found my new calling. I had a tremendous sense of accomplishment and, although I did end up killing, I felt absolutely no remorse. I freed up a mother and daughter from living in fear after bringing them back together.

As a SEAL I always knew that we did what we had to do and accomplished, many things. Often there were residual bad feelings about what I had done to complete the mission. This was vastly different.

I relaxed the best way I knew how. I trained twice a day to ensure not only my strength was good but that my martial arts and contact skills remained solid. I still enjoyed challenging myself the way we always did when I was in the teams. Of course, there we had each other to push and prod and even spar with. There were very few sparring partners that would be any help to me at the stage I was at now. I was still able to disarm and disable multiple attackers at the same time and I had no intention of losing that talent.

It took a few weeks before Alex, Norie and me were able to get out for lunch but eventually we did. I was pleased that Norie suggested one of my favorite spots, Duke's right on the sand next to the Huntington Beach pier.

It was one of my favorite restaurants. I used to love running into the real Gidget there, the mom of my surfing coach Dukey.

We met at the front door at the same time and were shown to our table that sat directly adjacent to the bike path and the silky white sands of Huntington.

We had just ordered drinks when I noticed a sign saying that Ruby's Diner was closing. I was shocked. Rubys had been there sitting like a beacon on the end of the pier for as long as I remember. Sure, there were a vast number of "better" restaurants where one could enjoy great food and drink, but I was always wanting the authenticity and history of places like Ruby's and Duke's. They were part of the fabric of Huntington to me. Turned out it was the same for all of us as we shared story after story about the pier itself and Ruby's.

Sure, Huntington Beach has changed over the years. The city has a higher crime rate than 62% of California's cities and towns. In Huntington Beach you have a 1 in 44 chance of being the victim of a violent or property crime. Of course, it was highly unlikely that I would ever be a victim, but you never know. I suppose there might be someone around who might give me a run for my money.

Huntington is still my beach and likely always will be, even though I now live in Newport Beach. It's odd when you think about it. I will leave my own neighborhood, with a great beach, to drive up to Huntington and surf there or just hang. I think a lot of it ties into my history with the town and the whole vibe of that section of oceanfront. A lot of people find it touristy, but I don't mind that. It makes for some good people watching.

Once we were done sharing a few stories, and a margarita or two, Norie asked if I enjoyed what I had done for Becky. I told her how rewarding it was and how great it made me feel, better than I had felt in years. Happier
than I had felt in years.

Norie and Alex exchanged knowing smiles, so I knew something was up and we were not just here to swap a few stories. Norie said that with her being high up in the Los Angeles District Attorneys office that she often heard of situations like I had just fixed. One spouse or the other disappears with a child, often to a country with no extradition treaties with the US. Sometimes they create new identities and try to remain in the states but that is more challenging.

It was easy for a spouse to claim an overseas trip was a vacation to secure the agreement and required paperwork from the other spouse. Once back in what was usually their own country however, all bets were off.
Diplomatic channels were typically ineffective and legal ones were hit and miss as well. Many other countries have too much corruption in government and/or the police forces so people of means can easily stay hidden.

Alex pointed out what she had just done for me to get Alyssa back home and said that with the power she possessed we could do so much more. It would be nothing connected to the ADA's office as that would put Norie in a bad spot and limit or eliminate her chances of taking over for Jackie Lacey when the time came. Jackie was one heck of a District Attorney and Norie aspired to follow in her footsteps. She would still be able to provide lots of intel as well as people for me to contact.

With what my aunt left me combined with my pension from the Navy I really didn't need money. Jonathon's investing tips had made me millions, literally, so I was set, but it's always nice to have more. It's also always nice to feel you are contributing to the betterment of society.

Norie said she was aware that the spouse from whom the child was abducted often paid well into six figures for a safe return. Alexis said that she would be able to arrange all types of travel, connections, and support for me as an independent agent of DHS.

She said I might need to do some side work and gather intel for Homeland Security on some of these missions but that would be a minor inconvenience for me at worst.

By the time our lunch was complete we had all agreed this would be our little project for the foreseeable future. Norie even mentioned a couple of names of people who had tried multiple legal and diplomatic approaches to retrieve their children. I filed both names away and said I would be back in touch.

Alex said that it would be easiest if we reviewed which country a child had been taken to so she could cross-reference any possible contracts I could work for DHS. It would be much simpler to arrange transport that way as well as many other details including in-country support and back up plans.

It was also more likely that Alex would be able to help arrange transport back to the US in these situations.

Chapter Twelve – Back To Mexico

Norie passed along a name of a lady who could use my help. She had arranged for us to meet at a local restaurant close to the neighborhood in which she lived. The Los Angeles basin is huge with city bordering city for miles and miles, each separated by only a street in most cases. It is a massive conglomeration of housing with everything from multi-million-dollar mansions to little more than hovels.

Typically, various ethnicities had settled into their own almost homogeneous neighborhoods within these cities. Over the last twenty years though, the lines had blurred. Wealth became more spread out and did not run along the lines of race or color, so neighborhoods were slowly becoming more integrated. Depending mostly on average income, each area had a pre-determined caste system.

You could have two cities bordering one another and while one had an active PTA and all the trappings you might expect the other might have gang skirmishes. Gardena, where Juanita now lived was one of those areas. Although sandwiched between the gang problems and crime in Inglewood (home of the LA Forum) and the even-more-serious issues in Torrance, Gardena was a nice little city.

Gardena had a healthy mix of ethnicities mostly living in harmony. It is known as the city with the highest percentage of Japanese people in California. At just a shade over 61,000 residents it was large enough to maintain its own culture. It is known as The City of Opportunity.

The average household income in Gardena has risen by over 50% in the last ten years and now shows 60% of its population with an income above $50,000 and almost 20% now earning above $100,000.

We all met and when I shook Juanita's hand, I immediately liked her. She turned out to be a pleasant and positive person. That was right up until she began to tell me about her son, now 7 years old, Jose Luis. Her face turned sad and sullen and the brightness she displayed earlier quickly disappeared. She began to tell me her story.

Juanita and Juan (how cute is that?) had purchased a house in Gardena when they were first married, and Juanita now owned that home herself. She got the house and full custody of her two children in the divorce. She had discovered that Juan was somehow connected to the cartels in Mexico, and she filed immediately for divorce.

Juan reluctantly granted it to her and signed over the house, and the kids, along with leaving her a couple of "clean" bank accounts that contained a total of more than three million dollars. Turns out he was far more successful than she had ever known.

He guaranteed her the money was good and could never be traced back to anything illegal. Apparently, Juan was putting his accounting degree to good work for one of his childhood friends.

Juanita had been married to Juan for only two years when they had their first baby. His name is Jose Luis, named after her husband's grandfather.

They had a second child about two years later, a little girl they named Serafina. Serafina was still with Juanita, but Jose Luis had been kidnapped a year earlier. She knew for certain that it was her ex-husband, now living back in Mexico who had him taken from her.

She had recently become aware that he was living in the Durango province. It is a sparsely populated area of about 1.9 million people spread out over more than 100,000 square kilometres. It was located Northeast of Mazatlán, inland, bordering the Sinaloa region, an area with which I was very familiar.

As we spoke and Juanita elaborated on what she knew it became clear I was her last hope. She had hired a private investigator to dig up information and discovered that Juan was working with the Sinaloa cartel made famous by El Chapo. They are a very scary and well funded drug cartel with a net worth between two and four billion US dollars. This would not be a simple retrieval as I knew this group very well.

With El Chapo again in custody I knew the cartel was being run by Ismael Zambada, also known as El Mayo. These were not people one messed with too often, as killing to them, had become a hobby. The good thing was that I already knew that organization and I was also aware they kept their finances isolated. More importantly, the people handling their finances, like Juan also operated in a bit of a bubble. They were structured to protect their wealth from rival gangs, a corrupt legal system and each other.

Not a lot of trust with these folks. Juanita explained that she had tried everything to retrieve her son from Mexico but knew nothing was going to work. The government would not help because she could not prove that Juan was the kidnapper.

She was at her wit's end and was about to give up hope when she got the call from Norie. She explained that she was prepared, if she retrieved her son, to move immediately and assume a new identity in a different city, even a different state if that is what was required. I got some more details and we parted with an agreement for her and I to meet at this restaurant in exactly one week. I knew I had to rough out some ideas and then go to Alex and see if she could help me.

Her Department of Homeland Security was not active within Mexico as things had been strained between the two governments for a while. That being said, I knew for certain there had been operations staged in Mexico over the last couple of years. I hoped there was something current, something I could be "hired" to as a contractor to help my cause.

The PI Juanita had hired learned that little Jose Luis usually spent four days each month at a coastal camp. I assumed this was likely when his father handled cartel business and met with whomever he needed to in order to salt away their ill-gotten gains. While the Mexican government was making a big deal about cutting down the cartel business there was still quite a bit of corruption at both city and state level, and even nationally I would expect.

I would have to deal with quite a few adversaries in order to rescue Jose Luis. Thankfully, he was a little older now and would be able to understand what I was trying to accomplish.

Chapter Thirteen – The Plan

By the time I met with Juanita again I had fleshed out a solid plan with a number of backup plans in case things went sideways. I had no choice but to continue to live by the Boy Scout motto and ensure that I was fully prepared.

Of course, I could not chance sharing any details with her. She agreed and I explained that she would be contacted and picked up by someone and moved to a new location while I was enroute. She would need to be fully packed, have everything in order and be ready to leave on a moment's notice. I could not tell her who would be picking her up as I needed to meet with Norie and Alex once more first. I was reasonably certain that Norie would not be able to help so all my cards were in Alexis' hand.

I had left Juanita with instructions to leave her bank accounts open but to convert the bulk of her cash to bearer bonds. We would arrange to transport those to her once she was established in her new home. While she was reluctant to leave all her friends and family behind, she knew it was the only way to get her son back and keep him safe. Her dirtbag criminal of a husband had left her with no other choice.

On the good side of things, again according to the PI, the cartel for whom Juan worked were unaware that Jose Luis was his son.

He had set it up so that everyone around them and whomever they met knew Jose Luis as the son of the housekeeper. As near as I could tell this story was 100% solid and even backed up by birth certificates and other critical information.

I was worried about one aspect of extraction. I would most certainly be operating outside the bounds of any agency that could help facilitate our return to the US. Overall, extraction was a huge concern, as it always had been.

I left Juanita with instruction to stick absolutely to her routine. There was no way to be sure that the cartel or Juan did not have eyes on her. It was time to lay the groundwork for my plan but first I had to speak with Alex.

The three of us got together at my house to discuss some of the details and find out who could help where. I could trust either of these women with my life so had no concerns about confidentiality here. I laid out the details of how Jose Luis was at water camp once a month. The good news is that Durango was closest to Mazatlán so I hoped I could use the fact the area is usually jammed with tourists in my favor. Norie was well aware that I knew intimate details of the cartels and that region so she would support with whatever I wanted.

I felt comfortable that anyone who might be able to recognize me was either dead or in jail by now, but I would still have to plan as if someone might spot me. I had caused a great deal of damage during my last foray into Mexico with the cartels, and they had long memories.

I was still contemplating how best to make my exit from Mexico once I had Jose Luis in hand. A water escape, up the coast had served me well in the past, but it would be more difficult to remain under the radar.

Moving inland might allow me to exit into one of California, Arizona, or Texas. While the borders are well guarded, Trump's ridiculous "wall" was nowhere near complete, and DHS would be able to help me anyway. I needed to confirm with Alex what would be the best approach.

We sat down and hashed through a lot of options and contingencies we would need to allow for. While Norie could not offer much directly she was helpful in reviewing plans and details we would need to handle. She would also be able to secure Juanita's bonds and transport them to her at a new location. Alexis would be able to closely monitor everything around Juanita's family and friends in California so it was possible she may be able to move back at some point. It was a faint hope that could happen, but hope, nevertheless.

Alex suggested that we might want to run a decoy inland and use the water, and the Coast Guard or Navy to get out. There were always ships up and down that coast sailing in international waters so I would need only to get to one of those. It added a certain complexity to my mission as I would then be on a timeline specific to the ship I needed to meet. There was also the issue of having to leave Mazatlán and go deeper into Mexican waters prior to being able to head North towards the international border.

I would prefer to cut across Baja California but that would require additional resources. It would also keep me on Mexican soil that much longer and that was not going to be a good plan. Transporting a nine-year-old boy with me would also add some challenges.

On my own, I could move easily under cover of darkness or even during the day and quickly neutralize any threats. I could not allow Jose Luis to see any of that type of thing. We finally agreed that, while I would prefer overland, it would be safer and simpler to head out to sea from Mazatlán. I could basically sail straight West past San Jose del Cabo and either meet a ship or make a run up the coast.

Unbeknownst to politicians, and even some of the highest-ranking people in the Navy, sometimes things were done outside the rules.

I felt this would be one of those situations and believed it was time for me to contact the Secretary of the Navy, Thomas Harker.

Even though Thomas W. Harker was appointed by Trump, a man I despised, I knew SECNAV was in my corner. I had met Harker a few times and had helped him out of a jam. I cannot say what that jam was but. Let's say, he likely owes me his life and most definitely his current position. A direction from SECNAV to an Admiral or Captain, or anyone else for that matter, was like getting a message straight from God in the Navy.

My next step was to contact SECNAV and see if there was a ship timeline that would mesh with mine. I didn't go to this well often, but he always stepped up if he was able.

Chapter Fourteen – SECNAV Support

I contacted Tom via secure email. Many people think the Secretary of the Navy must be military but that is not the case. In fact, the Secretary must be at least five years removed from any military service. What almost nobody knew about this particular secretary was that, like me, he was a former SEAL. He had a lifelong connection to us, and it was while he was a SEAL that I had helped him. That was how I ended up with a private, secure email to enable me to contact him.

We arranged to meet at my house as it was easy for him to slip away from his protection detail. He enjoyed driving his convertible, a little Triumph TR 6. It was a beautiful restoration of a great British sports car. I had found out that car was a gift he received from someone he had saved during his time. We never talked about it, but I knew that to be the case.

We shook hands heartily when I opened the door, telling him how being SECNAV agreed with him. He looked in great shape and in great spirits. He said he was simply happy to give back. He was also someone I could trust with my life, so I laid out for him what I was doing. I explained everything had to be off the books and I would be operating without support or cover.

He briefly tried to talk me out of it.

I gave him a couple of possible timelines and he said that the USS Detroit, our fastest Navy cruiser, may be sailing in international waters close to that time. It was based out of Jacksonville, Florida.

This was the fourth ship in the Freedom Class of cruisers and was the fastest. It was quite a departure for the US Navy as it was powered by water jets, like the Seadoos are! It has a wee bit more power though thanks to 2 Rolls Royce 36-Megawatt gas turbines and two diesels powering the four RR water jets. The sailors on it call it a giant jet ski. It is capable of 40 knots, about 46 mph, which is amazing for an almost 400-foot-long ship.

I would certainly be safe if I could get us to that ship as it is equipped with some serious armament. It has a Hellfire missile system, airframe missiles and a 57 mm gun along with many other surprises.

Tom said that I would need to get to international waters, disable whatever boat I was on and then be "rescued" by the ship. I would have complete paperwork for myself and Jose Luis indicating our US citizenship in case we needed it. For the most part however, we would remain under the radar. That was assuming I could even get us there.

Tom left our meeting with a hearty handshake and a hug telling me he was glad he could help out. I was to leave the details to him and gave him my satphone number to be sure he could advise me of the timing to hook up with the ship.

Now it was time to implement my plan. I had three weeks to get in place before Jose Luis would be on the coast. I needed to get there, locate a boat, and ensure that everything would be ready. The key would be the sailing schedule of the Detroit of course as that would be only way out once we were in that boat.

Chapter Fifteen – Final Preparations

I made my way down to Mexico and settled in close to Durango. I was not able to bring weapons with me but had made arrangements to pick up a few of my favorites once across the border. I couple of garrottes, two ka-bar knives and, of course, two beretta pistols. Just in case, I also had a long range 50 calibre sniper rifle that I was proficient at kill shots with from as far away as two kilometres. I wasn't quite "armed to the teeth," but I was close.

I was encamped in a small shed hidden in the desert and felt safe I would remain undetected. Once I began to scout around for boats, I was ecstatic to find out there was a 50-foot Mystic in the marina at Mazatlán. It was the same as the Miss Geico, one of the fastest boats in the world. It was designed specifically for offshore racing and could handle just about anything.

It weighed almost 12,000 pounds and was built of carbon fibre and Kevlar. It carried two Lycoming turbine engines and was capable of more than 200 miles per hour. I suppose you should be able to go fast with 3,700 hp pushing you! Luckily for me the boat was often rented out for rides by the rich and famous. That was ideal because a boat like that required two pilots, one on the throttle and one steering.

I had my boat and now I had to ensure that I could accomplish what I needed to.

I reviewed the schedule of when Jose Luis would arrive at Mazatlán and was pleased it synched up with the sailing plan of the USS Detroit. Now I just had to book the boat. I would pose as the security for a Hollywood star who wanted to remain nameless and scheduled a test drive with them for the day the Detroit would be closest to that coast.

I knew that the boat carried an inflatable dinghy on board and some serious PFD's too, along with shark repellent weapons. I would direct them where I needed to go and when we got close, I would give them the drugged water I would bring.

I would explain that the boy was my son, and this would be his only chance to get a ride in one of these. I had my schedule and all the required details including a locator program on my cellphone that would allow me to track the Detroit.

It would be a matter of grabbing Jose Luis, getting to the boat as quickly as possible and getting in the sailing line of that ship. Once they got close enough, I would shoot up a distress flare and that would hopefully be it.

Chapter Sixteen – The Grab

I was regularly driving into town in the Jeep I had so that I would not look out of place. I needed to be able to move freely once I had the boy and being seen often was the best approach. I fit in quite well as I looked like any other tourist. According to the schedule I had I was expecting the boy to be there the following day.

I had to leave him one additional day and then grab him later in the evening. The boat would get us out to the ship early the next morning. The seas were looking to be smooth so top speed wouldn't be an issue. I slept off and on the evening before as I was always a bit on edge during any mission, in or out of the Navy!

I drove into town the next afternoon and swung by the marina where Jose Luis was supposed to be. I waited for an hour until I finally got a glimpse of him. He had two guards close the whole time I watched but there could have been another one being used for overwatch. There was no way to be certain of that until I made my move.

They left and I followed them at a safe distance back to the house where they were staying. I remained close the rest of the night monitoring any people coming and going and watching for any other guards.

There appeared to be one more in the house and I wonder if that wasn't Juanita's ex husband. I couldn't be certain but that didn't matter anyway.

No matter what I did or how I handled this he would assume his ex-wife had taken Jose Luis. That was why we were setting her up with a new identity and location for at least a couple of years. Her family and friends would be closely monitored.

As I thought about this, I decided to slightly alter my plan. We would still take the boat, but I would leave enough breadcrumbs so that it would appear that we had been killed in the boat. They would be able to discover that a woman took Jose Luis out on that boat, but it exploded at sea, with no survivors. It was no guarantee they would not search for the boy, but it might shorten the time they would search.

I didn't want to kill innocent people, or anyone else for that matter, so I would need to take control of the boat. It could be handled by one driver as long as you were not operating at top speed. I would get them to stop the boat and then draw my gun and set them adrift in the dinghy with life preservers etc. Once I was on the ship, I could send an SOS with their location.

I left my shed in the hills later the next afternoon. I was nicely rested and ready to go. I had confirmed the boat for early the next morning and knew exactly where we were heading. I had discovered a sailboat in the same marina that was unattended. It turned out it was some rich American who kept it there and only used it a couple of times year. This was not one of those times.

I parked in the trees away from the house and then set myself up close by so I could monitor everything. I watched through my binoculars all the goings on in the house. Finally, I saw Jose Luis going up to what I assumed was his bedroom with a lady. She came back downstairs and left about a half hour later.

I waited another hour checking each window and looking at the surrounding area. There were cameras outside, so I assumed they had some inside as well. I had a full balaclava with me and slipped it over my head before I entered the grounds. I waited patiently next to the patio until one of the guards finally came out for smoke.

He spotted me but as he opened his mouth to call out the noise was suppressed by a blow to the side of his head. He was knocked cold, and I first zip tied his ankles and wrists and then gagged him tightly. I opened the door and as I turned the corner his partner was right in front of me.

He didn't go down quite as easily and when he actually landed a punch, I got a little perturbed.

I was just going to get him down so I could tie him up like his buddy, but I got a little mad. I danced around a bit and inflicted some severe damage on him as he swung wildly at me. He actually did not land another punch as I delivered kicks and strikes all over his body. A final roundhouse to the head put him down and out. I zip-tied him just like his buddy and then dragged the other guy into the house.

I put them in separate rooms and then went upstairs softly calling out Jose Luis's name. I opened his door as I told him his mother had sent me and he had nothing to worry about. I was caught by surprise when he ran up and hugged me. I took out my phone and showed him the recording his mother had made for him.

We went back to his room to gather a few clothes and treasures of his and we walked out to the Jeep. I told him he would be with his mother tomorrow, he just had to be brave and stick with me. He reached out and tentatively grabbed my hand. As I walked around the jeep to get into my side, I felt a hard blow to my back. Fortunately, it landed below my head and neck, and I was just staggered.

I spun around in ready mode so I could set myself against the attacker. He had a knife in his hand, but I could see he was nowhere near as skilled as I was. He lunged at me with the knife, coming surprisingly close to making contact. I trapped his arm against my body and twisted his wrist until the knife dropped as I heard his bone snap. He yelled out once, but a short elbow driven into his jaw silenced him.

I was mad at myself for not checking further and making the assumption there had to be another guard somewhere. I tied him up like his buddies and left him immobilized in the living room. By the time the lady who was here found them, we would either be on the Detroit or awfully close to it.

I told Jose Luis to crouch down in the back as I drove us to the marina.

It was closed and there was nobody about, so we got to the sailboat uneventfully. As we walked inside, I decided calling it just a boat was a disservice. This was a serious sailing yacht. I could see myself living on something like this.

I checked over every inch of it and marvelled at the multiple staterooms, heads, and a very well-equipped galley. There were only staples there like dry foods but that worked fine. We each had a bowl of oatmeal before settling down in bed.

Chapter Seventeen – The Open Sea

My alarm went off at 5:00 AM and Jose Luis was none too impressed when I woke him. I explained we were first going on a really nice boat and then we would be getting on a big Navy ship on our way to his mom. He was surprisingly calm as I described what we would be doing. I asked him if he had any questions and he said he just wanted to see his mom and then he thanked me for getting him out.

We got to the dock at precisely 6:00 as had been agreed. I was pleased to see the two pilots already waiting with the boat opened up and idling. It took some cajoling, but I got them to agree to allow Jose Luis to come with us. Before we stepped onboard, I admired the twin power plants and asked the guys about them. I needed to put them at ease to give me the element of surprise.

I gave them the coordinates of where I wanted to go and where we would be taking my bosses. I swore them to secrecy but told them I was working for George and Amal Clooney. That seemed to really get their interest, they were probably thinking of Amal in a bikini or something. The more relaxed they were, the easier this would be on everyone.

We stepped into the cockpit, and they showed us all the emergency gear before we all got strapped in.

The captain went to the back and closed the motor hatches and then strapped himself into his seat. Our seats were between and slightly behind the two pilots. The throttleman seat was on the port side and the pilot was starboard.

They said that way they could get the best angle of sight. The craft was equipped with radar, sonar, and a few other goodies too so I had no doubt there was a GPS locator system on it. That would help with my cover story as when the boat blew up it would simply disappear.

I tried to delay a little by asking more questions as, according to my GPS watch, we would arrive too soon before the ship. I didn't want to sit dead in the water for too long. I succeeded in asking enough dumb questions to get the time I needed. Finally, we idled out of the marina and off into the big, blue sea.

They said we would first run it at only 70 miles per hour to get everything warmed up. I recalled that, even as a SEAL, I had never gone that fast on water except for my last foray into Mexico. Of course, I was no longer an active SEAL at that point in my life, so I was on a private boat.

They dialed in the coordinates and then lit it up. Almost immediately we were skimming the tops of the slight chop at over 180 miles per hour. It was ridiculous. We were going faster than any single, or dual, engine helicopter at that point and it was blowing my mind to be honest.

I watched in the mirror as Mazatlán quickly disappeared behind us transitioning to a mere dot on the horizon. It seemed like it had only been minutes when I looked right to see Cabo San Lucas. The tourists on the beach appeared tiny as we passed by in a blur.

Jose Luis looked a little scared, so I calmed him down by saying how much fun this was. It was indeed a LOT of fun.

As we approached where the ship was going to be in a little while I asked the boys to shut it down for a bit so we could take a look around. They reluctantly agreed, no doubt thinking it was a bit strange. I kept Jose Luis belted in as I unstrapped and prepared myself.

As I stood, I one-punched the throttleman into darkness and then spun and dropped the flabbergasted captain. I zip-tied both of them and then grabbed the inflatable raft bag along with the life jackets. I needed to move quickly as I still had to travel at least ten miles to get in the path of the ship and shut down, leaving these two behind to be picked up later.

I explained to Jose Luis what I was doing as I dropped the lifeboat over the side and pulled the inflator string on it. It quickly began hissing and creaking as it inflated to full pressure in no time. I tied it to the boat and then went inside to get the two boys into life jackets and into the boat. They kept saying they were going to have me hunted down and killed so I spun around to the captain, grabbed his face, and advised him exactly why that would be a horrible idea.

He seemed to understand me, and they both got into the boat. I told them I would send a distress signal with their coordinates, and I was certain someone would be there soon. They had nothing to worry about provided they forgot they ever saw me.

I got back in, closed the hatch, and fired the motors back up. Although there were all kinds of switches and gauges, I had watched the captain start it the first time and it wasn't complicated. Switch on the fuel feeds, set the throttle to idle and then hit the starter switch for each motor, one at a time. I looked at the heads-up display and could see the Detroit on the far-left side of the radar screen. It was the only large signature, so I figured it had to be the Detroit.

I had to lock the steering wheel straight ahead while I went over and adjusted the throttle after putting her in gear.

I would need to perform the operations in reverse when we got close to where I wanted us to be "found." It was a little tricky as these things were never designed to be operated by only one person.

The boat was a much rougher ride in the open sea at only 50 Miles Per hour but I did not want to risk going any faster. I needed to ensure that once I shut the boat down that I was close enough to the Detroit's path for them to spot my flare, so I kept a close eye on the radar.

Once there I would also have to rig the charge that I had ready in my backpack. I would need to position the charge and blasting wire close to the fuel tanks to ensure the boat was obliterated once we were far enough away. I had it setup so I could trigger it from my phone so that would make it easy.

I contemplated asking the Captain to "demonstrate" one of the armaments for me but knew that every shell was accounted for on these sea trials.

Firing a missile at that boat would create far more problems than it might solve. I also was not aware of how much the Captain had been read in on what I was really doing. I suspected the broken-down boater approach was to provide a realistic cover story to everyone else on the ship. I just had to ensure that Jose Luis didn't say anything, so I had briefed him extensively on why he had to keep quiet.

I was about to cross the planned path of the Detroit, so I let us drift a bit and then I shut off the motors. As we were leaving the boat, I would switch on both fuel feeds to ensure the boat would be completely obliterated. I watched the radar screen until I could confirm with my long-range binoculars that the ship heading towards us was indeed the Detroit.

Finally, I could see the flag and, even from almost head on, the recognizable profile of the warship. I waited until they were about two nautical miles out as I knew it would take at least that to stop the ship. I fired two flares one minute apart and raised the boater in distress flag. It was a tense few moments, but I watched as the warship slightly altered its course to ensure it didn't swamp me.

Chapter Eighteen – Like Riding A Bike

Finally, the massive ship was resting in the water as close to me as was safe. I had paddles out and was paddling towards them as they threw a rope ladder over the edge. They used a bullhorn to tell me they would send someone down for us. I grabbed the horn in the boat and yelled up that I could get us up. I could see the look of confusion on the seaman's face as he saw there were two of us. He likely figured the boy was too small to use the ladder himself and too large for me to carry.

I would have to scramble all the way up to the flight deck as the much closer, waterborne mission access doors, were apparently not functioning. Those are quite close to the waterline and typically used for launching attack boats for SEAL-type landings.

He had no idea who he was picking up though. I told Jose Luis to hold onto my neck as I lashed him to me with a belt. I easily scrambled up the rope ladder and watched the group at the edge of the deck increase in size as word got around. By the time I stepped onto the deck and stood Jose Luis on it there were no less than fifteen people applauding me. Rather good audience when you figure the whole ship only carries about 50 crew.

The Captain reached out his hand to shake mine and said, "welcome aboard sailor. Glad we could be of help."

I replied, "Thank you very much Sir, I'm glad you were close by." Our secret needed to remain a secret as it could even blow back on SECNAV, and I certainly did not want that to happen. I really wanted them to be aware I was a SEAL but that had to remain my secret.

As we steamed towards Florida, the Captain was kind enough to show us around his ship. It was very impressive. The Detroit is a newer class of warship designed to fulfil multiple tasks, depending on what the situation required. The bridge looked a lot like a video game with joysticks everywhere controlling the ship's systems and propulsion.

At 389 feet long and a 57-foot beam it was an impressive and fast warship. Sometimes hard to imagine that a 3,400 metric ton ship (that's over 6.8 MILLION pounds) was propelled by four water jets. Highly maneuverable and with only a 14-foot draft it could go virtually anywhere and annihilate its targets. Jose Luis was loving the tour and so was I.

It wouldn't be long at all until we were docked safely in Florida. I waited until we were at least ten miles from the boat before triggering the charges. It was a cloudless sky and calm seas so as I looked out the stern of the ship, I was able to spot a plume of black smoke. Hopefully, nobody was close to it when it blew.

I also sent the approximate coordinates of the lifeboat with the two operators in it to the local authorities. I was sure they would be fine.

Once retrieved they could also confirm who was on the boat with them and the fact it blew sky high as I was sure they would have spotted the plume of smoke as well. That was the advantage of leaving the two fuel pumps on as the boat itself would have been flooded with AVGAS. That's all that type of engine could run on, and it was super volatile.

Chapter Nineteen – Home At Last

We cut across the Gulf Of Mexico at speed and then turned North after we rounded Key West. Jacksonville is at the top Northeast corner of Florida, so we were able to see quite a bit as we steamed that direction. Finally, we were easing smoothly into the dock at Naval Station Mayport. NS Mayport is the third largest naval facility in the US with room to accommodate 34 ships. It also has an 8,000-foot runway capable of handling most aircraft in the DOD. It really brought back some strong memories for me as I stood on deck while the Captain berthed his ship.

Across the bay was another ship of the same class as the Detroit. It was actually a Trimaran, a ship that had three interconnected hulls. They are very stable and also amazingly fast. It was a stealth design, so it looked very sleek and sinister as it sat at dock. I knew I could spend days staying here and seeing all the new ships, but we had to leave quickly.

The Captain came to us and led us off to a waiting car. There were not too many words spoken but as he closed the door of the car for us, he saluted and added a simple, "Godspeed sailor." I saluted right back and then sent a message directly to Tom letting him know we were safe on the ground, and everything had gone smoothly. I thanked him profusely for his efforts and risking his reputation to get us back here. He replied with a simple, "Think nothing of it, glad I could help."

I had been in contact with Alex, and she had already set up Juanita in a hotel in Saint Augustine, which is just South of Jacksonville.

It would only be for a few days as Juanita and Jose Luis were going to eventually end up living just outside of Tampa. It would be easy for them to hide until it was confirmed that nobody was tracking her or watching any of her friends and relatives. Alex, thanks to all the software and monitoring systems at DHS, would be able to effortlessly keep tabs on everyone Juanita knew.

I parked the car in the lot after surveying the area and led Jose Luis to the room number I was given. I knocked softly on the door and then stood there as Juanita scooped him up and hugged him tightly. They were both crying as I closed the door and left them alone for the evening. I was in the room next door and, as per my usual after mission habits, fell into a deep and restful sleep.

I awoke to a soft knock on the door, and it was Juanita. She said that Jose Luis was still asleep, and she wanted to thank me for my efforts. I invited her in, and we sat and had a coffee while I gave her some of the details. I explained how we would be able to monitor her, and everyone involved with her, very closely and that I expected she would be able to return to her old life at some point. Unfortunately, I was unable to give her a timeline but said that Alex would keep in touch.

She gave me a great big bear hug as she thanked me once more and then handed me my payment in bearer bonds. I thought $250,000 would look like more but it really didn't look like much at all. Five measly pieces of anonymous paper worth $50,000 each. Bearer bonds were almost extinct in the US these days, but they could still be used.

Unbeknownst to the general public, governments still use them for situations just like this. The very reason the IRS hates bearer bonds, their anonymity and lack of registration, is the reason it still makes them useful in clandestine operations. I didn't much care as I would get the money into my investment account and Jonathon would turn it into even more money in no time, if his past performance was any indicator.

I decided to rent a car and take a leisurely drive across the country home to California. It was a great way for me to relax and unwind. I knew that as I meandered towards home through Alabama, Louisiana, Texas, and New Mexico that I had people to stop and visit with. I was already eager to see friends of mine, including a SEAL brother or two, who I hadn't seen in far too long.

Chapter 20 – Trip Down Memory Lane

As I drove through Alabama, I realized I was excited to get to Louisiana. My average speed had picked up the closer I got to the Louisiana border. I had already decided that, as much as I wanted to see Travis and his family, I needed to stop in New Orleans on my way to Baton Rouge where the Master-Chief lived.

I always loved New Orleans, it was such a vibrant and alive place to be. It was a nice drive along the coast as well and I made really good time. I crossed into Louisiana and over the Maestri Bridge across Lake Pontchartrain feeling anxious but happy.

Route 11 was a terrific way to get to New Orleans as the view when you transitioned off the bridge to the almost water level causeway was one of my favorites. Depending on the weather and the light, Lake Pontchartrain looked like a massive ocean from that perspective. Streams of light glinting off the tops of the small swells and boats scurrying across the water made for a great picture.

I sometimes thought it odd how much I enjoyed that view when off to the left was Breton Bay and even the Gulf Of Mexico. Of course, the lake wasn't even technically a lake.

It is a saltwater estuary that connects to the Gulf of Mexico and is the second largest inland body of salt water in the United States. Although it is 630 square miles in area it averages only twelve feet deep. The largest inland saltwater body in the US is, of course the great salt lake in Utah at 1,700 square miles.

I had booked myself into a quaint little hotel in the French Quarter called the Andrew Jackson Hotel. From the street side it looked like another architecturally interesting New Orleans house, but it was a boutique hotel. It was very well appointed for a three-star rating and had a nice courtyard where one could enjoy a morning espresso and a beignet. It was also a pleasant walk to Bourbon street, where all the action was. I needed to blow off a little steam and relax and Bourbon street was the best place to do so.

I rolled up to the hotel and quickly got checked in and grabbed my room key. It was still early but I decided I needed a nap, so I closed all the curtains, set the air conditioner, and got under the covers. I slept soundly for about three hours and awoke refreshed and ready to go. It was already 10:00 PM but I knew things were just getting started. It was time for a late dinner at one of my favorites.

Many people don't like Pat O'Brien's, but I love it there. Certainly not the best food in NOLA but a really fun place to be.

I got a table for two against one of the walls, ordered a hurricane, and proceeded to people watch. I ordered a poboy sandwich, which I knew they did well and just kicked back. When I was done, I went looking for some live music of which there is no shortage of in New Orleans.

I ended up at the Famous Door, a long-time Bourbon street music hot spot. It was just a great place to sip on a drink and relax. There was a pretty decent cover band paying who did about 50% of their own music and I was really enjoying it. I was quite sure I was sending off a "leave-me-alone" vibe but that can be difficult to do down here.

A couple of guys pulled up two chairs to my table and sat themselves down without asking. I said, "Hey those spots are taken. I'm waiting for someone." The one smiled at me and said they would move or perhaps stay when she got here. I chuckled a bit and said simply, "I wasn't interested." The other one looked me and said, "You might be, give it time."

I really wasn't in the mood for this kind of BS, so I snapped back, "Never gonna happen buddy. Now please leave." They looked at me as if they were ready to spit in my face and shoved off. They walked past a couple of times over the next three hours asking where my friend was. They even sent over a couple of drinks, which I promptly sent back.

It was now coming up on 2:00 AM and I felt like getting back so I cleared up my tab and left. Once you leave Bourbon street headed to where I needed to go there were a lot of tight, dark side streets and alleys. I was not at all worried but, as always, wary and paying attention. I heard two sets of footsteps that sounded like they were getting closer as I turned onto a darker street. I decided to cut through an alley and that was when one of them yelled out, "it's not safe for a good-looking woman to be in these alleys alone at night."

I think it surprised them when I stopped, turned around and stood there smiling. "I'm not too worried, I can take care of myself." The taller one smirked and said, "Maybe we'll take care of you honey. You know give you what you were looking for in the bar." In the politest voice I could muster I said, "Look, I don't want any trouble here and you really don't want to try anything with me."

The shorter guy, who was the more muscular of the two, laughed out loud, glared at me, and said, "Maybe, we'll just do whatever we want." I laughed right back and said simply, "Not likely." That was when they both began to move toward me. They closed the gap a little more quickly than I expected but I still would prefer to get out of this by talking.

"C'mon fellas, I'm sorry if I insulted you. I didn't mean to. I'm just trying to relax." The taller guy said it was too late for that and he reached for me. I knocked his hand away and told them I did not want any trouble and they should just leave me alone. The stockier one said, "You have no purse and clearly nowhere to be carrying a gun so what are you going to do about it?"

I tried one last time. "I am a highly trained military person, and I am top level in multiple martial arts." Oddly enough, that turned out to be the wrong thing to say. The tall guy laughed and said his friend was an MMA fighter, maybe he and I should go. I reiterated one more time that I didn't want trouble but as he took off his jacket, I knew there was no way out.

I set my own jacket down with my phone in the pocket on recording mode for the last five minutes. In case I got caught I would need to have proof of what happened. He came toward me relatively weakly, clearly having no idea of what I could do and obviously thinking I was "just" a woman. He threw a couple of strikes I easily dodged and then attempted a kick to the outside of my knee.

I trapped his knee against my leg and delivered a quick kick of my own to his groin. I missed the target, but he still realized in that moment this was not going to be easy. I stepped back prepared as he stupidly started to move right back in, directly in front of me. I delivered a hard strike to the middle of his chest that staggered him.

Anyone with any common sense would have simply left at that point. Like too many of these mid-level guys he really thought that he could beat anyone in a street fight. He came in and attempted a direct shot to my face. I trapped his arm, twisted, and delivered a hard elbow to his jaw. I'll say this for him, he certainly did not have a glass jaw. He took the shot and stepped back and now he was in full octagon mode.

He tried a number of attacks which all failed. I drew him in close while blocking and dodging punches. As he leaned his head down slightly and readied for a kick, I grabbed him in a muay thai head clinch and delivered a knee to his mouth. The head clinch was where you locked your hands behind the target's head and then used that as leverage to elevate yourself and deliver the knee. It was usually a quick end to the fight. I was surprised his buddy just stood there with a dumbfounded look on his face.

He went down like a sack of potatoes, blood already spilling from cut lips and most certainly a missing tooth or two. He lay crumpled on the ground, and I looked at his buddy, "You can try your luck if you like but I'll do way more damage to you than I did to him." I walked past him and laughed as I faked a jab and he flinched and drew back almost running out of my way to tend to his comatose pal.

I took my time walking back to my hotel and cooling down on the way. I was unsure if I wanted someone to try that so I could get in a little scrap, or it was simply a happy coincidence.

Either way, I felt good about being me and quietly thanked the US government for all the training.

Chapter 20 One – Baton Rouge

After my incident in New Orleans, I was happy to be on my way to Baton Rouge. It was a short drive, but rather boring, in spite of all the views close by. Due to the flood potential and the level of the land they typically built high levees to protect it, so the road often did not have a view of the gulf.

It wasn't long before I was pulling into Travis's driveway in his suburb. Uncharacteristically, Travis came running out to greet me and hugged me as I got out of the car. I smiled at him, "great to see you again Master-Chief." He got a stern look similar to what he always had and said, "that's the last time you use that name. It's Travis or nothing now." He laughed when I said, "Well I suppose I COULD call you nothing but that doesn't seem very nice."

We were soon sitting in the backyard as he tended to his smoker, letting me know he had started a brisket late last night so it would be perfect when I arrived. I always liked Baton Rouge. It was a neat place. When I briefly considered returning to school my choice was the Baton Rouge campus of LSU. It was a great institution and the largest of the LSU school system.

He had already told me I was staying at least one night so we were two beers into the evening in short order. His wife was really nice, and he now had three kids, all girls! I have to admit I may have felt a little sorry for him.

Right up until his oldest Hanna, who was ten, asked me to show her a few moves. She proudly said she was going to be the next female Navy SEAL.

The look in her eye was an indication she might do just that. It made me feel really good to know that my service might inspire many more little girls to fulfill their own dreams.

Travis told her not to bother me, but I was down on my knees in two seconds showing her a few things. I was surprised to see she already had some surprisingly good skills, for any age, much less a 10-year-old. We did a few defensive moves and then we sat back down so she could tell me how much she liked muay thai.

My heart swelled when she told me she had a photo of me in her room. Travis added that it was a little hurtful that there was a photo of me but not of him during his days as frogman. His wife chimed in with a "who would want a picture of your ugly mug on the wall, "and then had a hearty laugh. The evening was wonderful and made me wonder why I had made some of the choices I did.

As I drifted off to sleep later that evening, I remembered that I liked what I was doing, and I really enjoyed my life. I'm just not sure that I am cut out to share a life with anyone. I did wonder what was next though.

I ended up leaving the next morning. As much as I enjoyed the visit and seeing Travis and the kids, I was getting antsy already.

Chapter 20 Two – Homeward Bound

I wound my way slowly across the country, stopping to take in many sights. I spent some time in Austin, Santa Fe and Tucson before dropping into Las Vegas as I meandered. I always enjoyed Vegas although I wasn't really much of a gambler, at least not a good gambler. I just liked being there and the fact that the city never seemed to close. There was always something going on somewhere.

I toured the Hoover Dam for the umpteenth time and visited many other touristy spots. As much as I enjoyed the trip, I felt a certain sense of peace as I finally crossed the state border back into California. It was home for me, and all that home brought with it. Another day and I was rolling into the driveway of my house.

I walked in the door, kicked off my shoes, and went out to lay in the sun on my patio. Smelling the salt air and feeling the Southern California sun on my skin was always relaxing for me.

Of course, it didn't take long for me to begin wondering who would need my help next? I was anxious to speak with Norie and Alexis. I jumped when my cell rang, and I recognized the voice. It was Tom Harker. I told him I was surprised to hear from him. He just said he would like to meet with me as we need to discuss something.

I said, no problem, and we set a time to meet at Huntington Beach. Of course, I suggested Duke's and that was where we agreed to have lunch. I needed to be there to really ground myself, convince my psyche that I really WAS home.

I rolled into the parking lot a little early so I could get us my favorite table. It was a quieter corner away from other tables, but you were still on the beach. It was your typical Southern California summer day. Clear blue sky and the bright sun warming your skin and glinting off the tops of small waves. I really could look at that all day long.

I heard a familiar voice and Tom sat himself down across from me. "You're looking well," he said. I returned the compliment. We ordered a couple of drinks and I asked what he had in mind. 'It's not like this is a purely social call, is it?" He nodded his head that it was not.

He leaned on his elbows on the table and leaned in, "I've been asked to do something, and I could think of nobody better than you." "What is it sir?" He laughed and said we didn't need to be so formal. He went on to warn me that once I was read in, everything we discuss was absolutely secret. I was still shocked when he laid out the situation.

He had been approached through back channels to assemble a team to retrieve children who had been abducted. These were situations where the kids were taken to non extraditable countries and there were no diplomatic options. While the USA could not be seen as treading on foreign soil unwelcome, if someone were able to operate under the radar that would be best. He said he knew of nobody better than me.

He then added that he knew what I had just done and had spoken with Alexis on a purely casual basis. He knew he could enlist her help as he had carte blanche from "the highest power" to do whatever it took. I was interested. If I could do my work with the blessing of our government that might make things a little easier. Unfortunately, that wasn't exactly going to be the case.

While he was given this directive to "get it done," ANY involvement from the US government, perceived or otherwise, would spell disaster. I said that I understood the situation and when he asked if I was in, what could I say. I told him that I would really like to have Norie's help as well as Alexis. He said that could be done easily. I said that I might need one final piece of the puzzle and asked about his connections to the FBI.

He said they were strong, so I mentioned Colin Sharpe. I explained that he was one of the best analyst/agents I had ever known.

Tom said he wasn't sure about that one, we would have to see how the first one goes. That was when he sprung the immediate requirement on me.

Chapter 20 Three – Working With SECNAV

Although not officially, I knew that from here on in that Tom would control almost everything I did. I was good with that as I knew I could trust him with my life. I had done so many times before, so why not now?

He went on to explain that my first case involved the son of a foreign diplomat who was a little more than simply a diplomat. That was all he would share as far as the father went. He gave me a name and other basics and said that he would speak with Alexis and get her on board, as well as lay out a few details.

Turned out the son had been grabbed by dissidents in Syria. Jeez, could he have picked a worse location? Bordered by Iraq, Turkey, Lebanon, and Israel it was a real middle eastern hot spot and not the easiest place in which to operate, nor escape from. At any rate, it wasn't like I could say no. We finished our lunch and parted ways.

I was no sooner in my front door than I started planning entrance and exit strategies. There were few options, and none would be simple. The US had a couple of what they referred to as "non-NATO allies" in the region. Israel and Egypt were the two biggest ones in the area and Jordan was too, but Jordan had lost some of its standing lately.

The other option for egress could be Cyprus but that would involve getting safely across the Mediterranean Sea. After all, it wasn't like I could exactly have a Navy sub pick me up on the beach or anything.

According to my discussion with Tom there would be situations where, if I could get to a ship close by, I would be accepted onboard with no questions asked. He went on to explain those would be rare. Okay, my work was cut out for me, and I needed to get things moving.

The son was 12 years old, and intelligence said he was being held somewhere in Damascus. Syria was currently a political mess with all kinds of bad things happening. I supposed the one help might be a refugee approach, although that would pose its own problems.

I already thought it was more likely to use Egypt as an exit point. The Saudis were not overly friendly these days and travelling as a woman there was still not easy. Luckily, I had a great deal of experience operating in and around Iraq and Iran, so I was familiar with the challenges.

While not the shortest or simplest way to go it appeared that cutting through Jordan and making the 1,000-kilometre trek to Cairo might indeed be my best option.

At least if I could get to Cairo, I could seek refuge at the US Embassy there. While Egypt was also a bit of a political shit-show these days, it was much less so than the surrounding regions.

I mapped out a large number of details and possible scenarios before meeting Alexis.

Chapter 20 Four – The Middle East

I had never had any intention of getting close to Iraq again but here I was planning to do just that. I had photos of the boy who had been taken along with some last known locations. While there was no official oversight of that area, satellites could still be tasked to zoom in for some stealthy recon.

I knew that from the city of Damascus I could take the M5 South to Amman and over into Jerusalem. A tourist cover was always best and the easiest to maintain. Plus, it would allow me to see some great sights like the Damascus Gate, which is the entrance to the old city of Jerusalem.

While it would add hours and kilometres to our escape it would likely be the safest. If I determined that getting to Cairo would be too difficult, I could always change my exit plan from there. The Italian Navy operated quite freely in the Mediterranean Sea, and I knew that SECNAV had a great relationship and good contacts there.

Certainly, heading through the Gulf of Aden, between Yemen and Somalia would not simplify things either so that was out right off the bat. The Middle East was a difficult place in which to operate.

Alexis and I met at a restaurant off the beaten path and began to discuss the overall situation and how we could pull this off. Alexis had gathered more intel for me and said the last known whereabouts of the boy was close to the Damascus National Museum.

The good news about that was that it is close to an entrance onto the M5 and also the Al Hijaz train station. Although the Hejaz railway was abandoned shortly after the First World War, parts of it still function today. Of greatest interest to me was the fact it ran from Damascus to Amman in Jordan. This might be the quickest and least disruptive way to travel but immediate situations would dictate my route.

Even though DHS had more power than anyone will likely ever know, Alexis said that travelling with standard weapons would be almost impossible. My best cover might be to travel as a religious tourist. There were always a lot of them in the area, even during troubled times and sometimes even more so because of troubled times. Again, my skin tone would be a positive and help me to fit in.

We decided my best entry into Syria would be from the South, coming up from Jordan. My cover as a religious tourist would be more believable coming from there anyway.

Alexis would have me set up with multiple passports from Canada, the UK and even a fully back storied Syrian passport. Unlike my past lives, I would be at greatest risk while simply travelling from point A to point B and not as much while in country.

I would be set up with access to a few different "clean" vehicles staged at various points on my journey. I would be able to switch vehicles easily and untraceably at strategic points so that I could travel at a pace that would not arouse suspicion. There would also be a kit containing passports for the boy that matched each of mine. There would be supplies to alter his appearance and a method to add the new look photos to the passports.

By the time we were done I knew exactly which spots might cause trouble and had an exit strategy for each. I would also be equipped with communication devices directly to an agent that Alexis would assign to keep watch on me. I, and the boy, would be tracked every step of the way as we made our exit. I knew that as soon as he was known to be missing all hell could break loose.

I decided I would take the boy soon after he went to bed. I would do my best to avoid having to neutralize people but if it could not be avoided, I would have to take lethal action. Every extra minute I bought myself before it was discovered he was missing would improve our chances of success.

I had a map stashed away and a local contact had confirmed the boy was now being held in a home on Al Hijaz street. That was North of the Hejaz Station and also the M5 entrance. I would not know which method of travel I would use to get him out until I was in country and could survey the landscape. I needed to get there quickly and knew I had to use commercial airlines as that would make it simpler to operate, at least before I grabbed the boy.

I prepared everything I needed and got ready to leave. I had packed all the traditional clothing women wear in that area. While Syria did not have dress regulations as strict as Iran, there were still considerations. For women, conservative should drive all your clothing decisions. I packed a few pairs of long light fabric pants, shirts that came right to the neckline and had long sleeves and also some vests typical of the area.

Women in Syria these days, at least in the big cities, can be seen wearing everything from the full abaya to more touristy clothes. The touristy clothes are not recommended outside of the large cities, however.

The abaya is the black long flowing dress-like covering from head to toe. They are multiple layers and women wearing that typically also wear the full face covering with only eye slits. I would stick to the less traditional look but wear a head scarf (Hijab) that would help me fit in.

It would be best to keep this fine balance between new and old as most of my travel would be outside the cities.

Conveniently, Arabic was one of the languages I could speak. Using Arabic would draw the least amount of attention to myself as that is what the majority of Syrians have as a first language. I had already been polishing up my conversational skills and was close to ready.

Chapter 20 Five – Back In Jordan

I was all packed and everything was in place for me, so I felt rather good as I headed to LAX. I would eventually be landing at the Queen Alia International airport in Amman, Jordan.

Queen Alia is the largest airport and the hub for Royal Jordanian Airlines. It was named after Queen Alia shortly after she died in a helicopter crash in 1977. She was Queen of Jordan and the third wife of King Hussein. She had been inspecting a hospital at Tafileh with the Minister of Health just prior to the crash.

Many think that if she lived longer that Jordan would have evolved much more quickly than it has. She was fully westernized and had a love of fast cars, water skiing and blue jeans. She had been educated at Hunter College in New York and fully embraced many aspects of American life. She was an agent of change much the same as Diana was in England and her loss was still mourned throughout the country.

My American airlines flight was uneventful and nothing much happened, thankfully. I landed in New York feeling refreshed thanks to a nice long nap on the plane. I was quite used to sleeping in a rope hammock or sitting in a side seat on military aircraft, so I always sacked out quickly on commercial flights.

There wasn't a huge delay before boarding my Royal Jordanian flight. All my identification worked perfectly, and I was moved through security at JFK without delay.

Although my flight would be only ten and a half hours, I had been booked in their Crown Class seats. Basically, it was a comfy bedroom in the sky if that is what you were after. The seats recline totally flat, turning into a cushy bed. As I had been dressed "in character" since LA I was really aware of the difference in how I was treated.

On American Airlines I felt very un-American to be sure. It seemed they were a little unclear on how to deal with me and there were also the looks I got from other passengers. I was not too impressed with my country and the way they made me feel. I couldn't even imagine how a real Syrian might feel in this environment. It really saddened me.

Once on Royal Jordanian it was the opposite. They were super respectful and treated me like I was a queen. I suppose the seats were appropriately named based on what I saw. I was served a delicious meal that included traditional food including appetizers of vine leaves, tabbouleh and shankleesh, and a main course that was like a five-star restaurant.

Tabbouleh is a tasty salad made with finely chopped parsley, tomatoes, mint, onion, and bulgur. It comes with a lemon juice based dressing and is designed to wake up your taste buds. Shankleesh is a type of seasoned cheese that looks a little like a rum ball. The food kept coming and by the time I was done I was definitely ready to sleep.

All the staff were outstanding, and I found myself awakened by a gentle hand on my shoulder. She whispered to me that we would be landing in about a half hour if I needed to do anything. I thanked her, grabbed my small travel bag, and headed to freshen up.

Alexis had arranged for me to have a driver at this point. She wanted to ensure there were no delays or issues getting me settled close to where they were holding the boy in Damascus. He would have a train ticket for me and a few other items I had asked to be provided. I learned I had a room booked for two weeks at the Four Seasons. It is in the central district of Damascus and would provide me with the most privacy.

I stepped out of the airport, and we spotted one another at about the same time. He greeted me and placed my bags in the trunk, and we drove off. My driver wished me well when he dropped me off at the train station and that was it. Someone else I would never see again. It was about a three-hour train ride from Amman to Damascus and I got settled in quickly.

I was able to sit in a tourist type car and enjoyed the views as I planned things in my head.

When I arrived, it seemed like I might have as many as seven days to get my mission started. I would survey the area around the house where he was being kept and determine some critical information about their schedules. It was unlikely they would be on high alert considering they were in Syria. It is not an easy place in which to operate, due to this level of vigilance, and successfully pull off a mission of this nature.

Stealth would be of the utmost importance. It's not like I could go in there guns a blazing and then have any hope of getting out with the boy.

I would need to quickly detail all the nuances including how many guards there were and things like shift changes. I slept soundly and left while it was still dark in the morning to locate the house. I was able to place a few tiny cameras in unobtrusive places that would let me keep a close eye on everything from a safe distance.

Before the sun rose, I was back in my hotel and getting everything set up.

I was pleased that everything worked and began to take notes as I watched. The boy had longer hair that was blonde so that would help me to disguise him. I would dye his hair black and make it curly and that alone would make him difficult to recognize.

After four days of scrutiny, I determined the guards were likely military. There were very precise shift changes with the male guards exchanging what looked like keys each time they met in the courtyard. There were also two females with them and the way one of them comported herself I had to assume she too was military or had at some point been military. She had that look about her and was clearly not someone you would challenge on a whim.

The men all carried weapons with holsters likely sewn into the jackets they always wore. The women appeared to be unarmed but I would prepare as if they were. So, I now knew there were two armed men, one woman who may be armed and one who was hopefully just a domestic.

I would not rely on that being the case and would prepare as if there were four people, I would need to get past, each well-trained and fully armed.

Fortunately, the shift changes happened just after dark and then another twelve hours later. I would hit them as close to the shift change as possible so I would hopefully then have at least ten hours before the boys' absence was discovered.

I readied everything for the following evening, including a couple of garrottes.

I would hope to get him out without killing anyone but if I needed to, I had carte blanch to do so. It's not like relations between the US and Syria could get any more strained anyway.

I had picked up the car that DHS had arranged for me, and I was all ready to go.

Chapter 20 Six – Grabbing The Boy

Morning arrived and it was like any other mission for me. Everything had been planned and I knew exactly what I had to do. I was as ready as I ever had been, just as if I were still a SEAL. You may not wear the actual trident after you left but it was always imprinted on your heart and mind. The commitment to freedom and the burning need to protect America and its citizens was ingrained. That never went away, and I was glad that was how it was.

I knew that no matter where I was or what happened that even a retired SEAL would NEVER be left behind. I found that very comforting, especially as I was now operating as a single person, no longer having a team of brothers to back me up. Sure, there was backup, but it would never provide the comfort nor the loyalty that you had with your brothers.

I drove and parked about a couple of blocks from the house where my car would just be another one sitting on the street. It would mean walking from the house to the car location, but I felt safer doing that rather than parking any closer. I watched and waited until after the sun set. The guards changed precisely on time once again and I waited another half hour. You never know if someone might forget something and return before the next shift change.

I was glad that on this team one of the guards smoked and one did not.

I had witnessed him go outside the back door and wander around the grounds as he smoked, no doubt telling those inside he was going to do a perimeter check. I knew I could subdue him quietly and quickly outside.

I would leave him there until I got to the others and then drag him into the house. I had my small backpack and had brought the scissors and hair colouring as I thought I might want to make the change before we left. I prepared my garrotte in case it was needed and positioned myself in some bushes close to the back door. I decided to take him as soon as he came outside as that would give me at least three minutes before any of them missed him.

I heard the door open, and I prepared myself. He had his hands in front of his face lighting his cigarette, so he didn't even see me coming. I delivered a hard front kick directly to the underside of his jaw and I was certain he was out cold by the way he fell. I drug him close to the house, gagged him tightly and zip tied his hands and feet together and then connected those two ties. He was effectively hogtied and would be almost unable to move or make any noise.

I waited patiently until the other guard stuck his head out and I grabbed him in a choke lock. I zip-tied him well and I put him down. As I began to stand back up, I felt a hard shot to the side of my ribs. The wind was knocked out of me, and I looked to see the woman adopting a martial arts stance. I was immediately buoyed with confidence as I was certain there was not a woman on the planet who could take me down.

We squared off in the kitchen as her partner watched from the floor. I had not seen the other woman yet, so I was hoping she was asleep and not phoning for backup. We traded a few strikes and then she left her right flank open with her guard held low, too low.

I faked a strike to the left side of her face as I delivered a debilitating kick to the right side of her jaw. I was certain it was broken as she was out before her head bounced off the floor. I quickly gagged her, and zip tied her and ensured the other guy was solidly tied up as well.

I crept quietly upstairs and found the woman indeed still asleep. I had determined it was unlikely she had any military training. She was sleeping soundly so I just gagged her, and zip tied her and then connected her to the bed.

I went to the boys' room and clamped my hand over his mouth and told him who I was and who had sent me. When I said I was taking him back to the USA his eyes lit up. He reached up and hugged me. I told him to pack some clothes and things in a bag and then to come downstairs. I left the woman upstairs where she was and then went to get the other two out of the yard.

There were some very large, heavy chairs in the living room. I took each of them, one by one. I sat them in a chair and then used my zip ties to affix their legs to the feet of each chair and their arms around the back. I pulled their arms through the space underneath the arm rest on each chair and connected them that way. It would make it far more difficult to escape.

I took the boy upstairs and quickly cut his hair and then applied the dye, packing everything into a zip lock we could dispose of on the way to the hotel. They might assume I would change his looks, or they might not. Might as well cover my tracks anyway I figured.

We got whatever we were taking and walked to the car through the alleys. In no time we were driving towards the hotel. I had originally planned to stay the rest of the night but determined I needed to change things. When they saw the precision with which I dispatched their team of guards there would likely be a large group coming after me.

The boy, Charlie, was quite happy and chatty the whole way. I think he was mostly happy to have someone to speak English with. He wasn't thrilled with the change in hair and color but when I explained it would help get him home, he was all in.

Chapter 20 Seven – Change Of Plan

The train back to Amman did not leave for another six hours. I thought that driving South on the M5 was what would be deemed the best route so decided that was not the way to go either. I got in touch with my DHS contact and advised I was changing the plan and heading to Beirut in Lebanon.

Not completely US friendly, I was hoping the Syrians would assume I would avoid that area. There were going to be some border challenges to deal with but so be it. There was an American embassy there, but the biggest challenge would still be the border. Even the slightest misstep could be deadly for me.

The largest border crossing between Beirut and Damascus had an almost 8 km "no-man's-land" between the two border stations. It would be worrisome to attempt to cross there. I knew that Hezbollah had opened an illegal border crossing through which they used to move fighters into Syria. They were allowing regular people to pass but I was worried that looking Syrian at that point would be no good.

I contacted my DHS liaison, and he secured an entry Visa into Lebanon for me and my "son." I would then be able to exit Syria and enter Lebanon through the Masnaa border crossing.

As the busiest crossing between the two countries, I felt that might be an aid. Knowing I would also have the proper paperwork, they might focus their efforts elsewhere.

I knew it was only about 60 km East from Damascus to get to the crossing. I could carry the kid on my back through the desert that far, if I had to.

There was no communication between the border points so I would use my Lebanese issued passport to cross. Alexis had also thought of all the options, so I had all kinds of paperwork for both of us. The good news was at the Lebanese border crossing money meant a whole lot more to those folks than laws.

Civil servants and military are paid extremely low wages and the struggles between the two countries have exacerbated the currency situation. For me, this was all a good thing. I knew that I could cross easily, especially when I left an envelope with two million Lebanese pounds on the seat, which is the equivalent of about 1,300 US dollars.

We drove calmly towards Lebanon in our Toyota Landcruiser. It was an older model and looked beat up, but it was mechanically perfect.

Toyota are the most popular cars in Lebanon and there are Landcruisers everywhere you look so it was the right vehicle. It was like driving a Honda civic in the states. We would arrive at the Syrian checkpoint shortly after sunup so there should be many other vehicles. They are typically anxious to see Syrians leave so I did not anticipate any issues there.

It had thus far been an uneventful drive and I was hoping that would continue.

The boy was dozing soundly in the seat next to me as I watched the sun begin to slowly rise over the desert-like rocky landscape. Fortunately, as you moved toward the coast the weather moderated. Once we were through the border crossing and into Lebanon it would be more like a typical Mediterranean climate. I was looking forward to feeling the ocean breeze coming inland.

As expected, we were detained very briefly at the Syrian exit. Typical inspection of papers and passports and ensuring the entry visa was paid and valid. That being said, the 8 km drive to the checkpoint into Lebanon still had me worried. There was absolutely nowhere to hide in that 8 km space.

Although I had all the required paperwork it was always a crapshoot at this type of border. You never knew what kind of corruption you might come up against or who may choose to detain you for no reason. Plus, being out in the open and completely unprotected was not a situation to which I was accustomed.

I was confident that the kidnappers were Syrian however, so it was highly unlikely they would have any Lebanese contacts who would help them. All the reasoning in the world didn't reduce my concern or second-guessing, however.

I suppose that was the nature of the beast. SEALs stayed alive and got everyone else out alive because we planned for EVERY contingency and possibility on a mission.

Finally, I could see the Lebanese checkpoint about a mile up the road and was glad to see cars ahead of me. You never wanted to roll in there as the only vehicle because they would detain you, inspect you and hassle you just for entertainment. There were armed sentries stationed at each side of the roadway and they appeared to be doing a cursory inspection as each vehicle passed. Nothing to be concerned about there.

We rolled slowly to a stop in front of an unkempt looking border guard. I was pleased he was not too chatty and likely did not live close to the address shown on our passports. We sat there for about five minutes while they checked the plates and took a closer look around the vehicle. They handed me back the papers and we were waved out of there.

I kept my eyes on the rear-view mirror in case any vehicle (official or otherwise) pulled onto the road behind us. None did but that did not reduce my concern.

I still had the envelope with the Lebanese money and decided I would give it away to someone deserving if I had the chance.

Chapter 20 Eight – Safe At The Embassy

The whole drive from Damascus was just a little more than two hours but it seemed much longer. The anticipation and angst around the two border crossings can take its toll on a person's psyche.

We were on Route 30 and had already passed Bourj Hammoud, which is just outside Beirut, and were now headed North to the embassy. We crossed the River of Death and hoped that name wasn't an omen. This part of the drive was rather nice as on our left for most of that portion was the Mediterranean Sea. The water was a unique blue in that part of the world, and I could watch the sun bouncing off those gentle waves for hours.

The embassy was not easy to get to. It was by the Awkar Municipal Building which also housed a farmer's market type place. I wanted to stop but I thought it would be silly to risk it. We were expected at the embassy and delaying would not be wise. We rolled up to the gates and showed our American passports and they swung open. We passed through and the heavy gates closed quickly behind us under the watchful eye of armed guards.

We were greeted by the US Ambassador to the Lebanese Republic, Dorothy Shea. She was only recently appointed by President Trump but had 28 years of experience in the foreign service.

She had also worked in Cairo, Jerusalem, and other spots. I knew she had a master's degree in National Security Strategy, so she understood the challenges around what I was doing.

Once we were inside, she advised that there had been bulletins issued regarding a "kidnapping." Fortunately, the only photos were of the boy, and he looked much different now than when I first acquired him. I felt relatively secure thanks in part to the papers I had received giving us multiple identities from multiple countries. I could simply select the safest one to use for the area I was in.

Beirut itself is an interesting place. It is the largest and capital city of Lebanon and is the center of commerce, business, and culture in the country. Unfortunately, much of its beauty was lost in lengthy civil wars but they have been rebuilding ever since. In 2009 the Times listed it as a top place to visit. I wished we could hang around but that would be far too dangerous.

I believed it would be safest to get moving as quickly as possible and to do so without letting anyone at the embassy know. While our embassies were generally never infiltrated there was always concern about information being shared with the wrong person.

Most US embassies were watched very closely and this one was no exception. I noted many options for enemy oversight the closer I got to the embassy.

I received a coded communication advising me that Tom suggested I move out the next day. There were a number of marinas at Beirut including both pleasure and fishing. I was advised there would be a pleasure boat and crew waiting for us at Le Yacht Club in Zaitunay Bay. It was one of the largest in the region and packed full of all manner of pleasure yachts and offshore boats.

Le Yacht Club had direct access to the open seas of the Mediterranean and would provide me with a quick getaway. The shores are always patrolled but there are many craft that run between Cypress and Beirut as well as to Italy and Greece.

As expected after my last chat with Tom Harker, there would be an Italian Navy boat operating close to us. Apparently, there was some sort of issue close to Cypress and Italy had dispatched two frigates to the region. It was not terribly out of the ordinary for the Italian Navy to venture that direction and a minor situation would be good cover.

I was contacted directly by someone who seemed to be just an embassy worker. Turned out she was CIA. She said that Tom had given her directions to get me out of there as soon as practical as the Italian frigates would be in the region for only the next 24 to 48 hours. It was about 230 km from Beirut to Cypress so the trip would be quick.

She advised there was a delivery every fourth morning from their seafood provider. The truck came from and returned directly to a fishing marina adjacent to Le Yacht Club. We would leave in a hidden compartment in that truck and then head to a boat at the club. Luckily, there was a lot of money in the area and these guys loved their go-fast boats.

Some of the inboard racers would have two or three 1,100 to 1,200 hp motors capable of speeds up to 160 mph. There were also quite a few high-speed boats used for sport and fishing. Those could have two to four outboards and travel at speeds up to 85 mph.

Once we were on the boat and away from the harbour, we could reach those frigates in as little as two hours! I was hoping for one of the slower centre-console boats to be honest. Those other high speed offshore racers were a really rough ride, especially at 140 mph! I was sure the boy wouldn't be impressed, and I didn't need a puking kid on my hands.

I prepared all our gear and told the boy what we were doing. He liked the idea of a boat, me not so much. Sure, I was a Navy SEAL and spent many, many hours in the water and on boats but there was also danger. If spotted or tracked, my escape, especially dragging a child behind was unlikely.

I slept very lightly, with every little noise putting me on alert. Finally, morning was close, and I was more than ready. Before sunup, the contact came to us and took us down some back stairs to the loading dock. The seafood was being unloaded and we were both crowded into a small compartment hidden between the cab and refrigerated part carrying the fish.

We were told to stay still and quiet no matter what and we felt the vehicle rumble to life and soon we were bouncing down the road. Fortunately, the marina was close. When we stopped, the compartment was opened, and we were handed a full set of gear that sailors typically wear. We even each had one of those self inflating, life saving life jackets. Even if you are unconscious, they keep your face pointed to the sky so you can breathe.

We followed the driver as he led us to the dock and pointed to a larger white, centre console boat idling at the end.

I chuckled a bit as we walked toward it and I spotted the name. It was a Greek boat named "LIBERTAS." She was the Roman god of freedom and the personification of liberty.

I liked that SECNAV had a sense of humor. I was glad he hadn't lost that since our days operating together. Besides the name, I also liked that the boat was one of the 85 mph centre-console boats as it would be a less violent ride.

The captain took our bags and buckled us into our seats. He said we would be travelling almost 200 kilometres to meet the frigate so it would take about two hours. He further advised the seas were calm so once we were safely away from the marina we would be flying smoothly across the Mediterranean.

I sat on the outside and admired the views and the colors of the sea as we moved away from the marina. I was glad for the sun and smooth waters when the captain began to ease the throttles forward. Soon we were skimming across the water barely feeling the small swells. The boy seemed a little nervous, so I reminded him where we were going. That brought a huge smile to his face.

True to his word, it was about two hours when the Italian frigates came into view. These were not huge navy ships; their frigates were of similar design to those used by other countries. I knew them to be of the Bergamini class and were like the constellation class frigates (FREMM's) used by our own US Navy.

They looked quite impressive when seen on patrol like this. The Italian frigates were about 470 feet long overall with a 64-foot beam and at 6,700 tonnes not a small ship by anyone's standards. As we approached closer to them, our Captain said we would be boarding the Carlo Bergamini.

He was the namesake of this class of frigates. He was an Italian Admiral who died at 43 years of age onboard the battleship Roma. I knew a great deal about the Italian Navy as I had been seconded to them for a period when I was a SEAL. They were all about history but then so are most navies.

I felt safe going to one of their ships. Once we were within about two kilometres of the ship, I saw a small transfer vessel coming around the stern of the Carlo. I explained to the boy what would happen next, and he seemed quite thrilled that we would soon be getting on this navy ship.

Once the tender was tied to us, the Captain tossed our duffels over into the small zodiac. The operator saluted me and helped us in as our old Captain wished us Godspeed. We sat on either side of the operator as he took us quickly back around the stern of the Carlo. We tied up on the Port side aft and climbed up a ladder tossed over the side.

Once we were on the ship we were greeted by an Italian sailor and taken directly below decks to a small room. It was setup with two single bunks and a small locker between them. We were told to remain in the room and that food would be brought to us soon. It was about a half hour later when I opened the door and was greeted by the boys' father.

The boy ran into his arms, and he thanked me over and over for saving his son. He said arrangements had already been made on commercial flights and I should get a good night's sleep. The young man turned and extended his hand to shake mine as he said thank you very much. Seemed very adult of him but I suspected he had already been through much more than what we just experienced.

That would be the last I would see of either one of them. The next morning, I was taken by helicopter to the Naval Branch Medical Clinic (BMC) in Souda Bay in Greece. It is a branch of the US Naval Hospital in Sigonella, Italy and I was familiar with it. I was taken directly to a private room and kept away from everyone.

An officer knocked on my door a couple of hours later and I was told I would be leaving just before first light on an aircraft headed to Norfolk, VA. I knew the distance to be roughly 8,000 km from Greece to Norfolk, so I didn't expect to be on a fighter or anything. I slept well that night and was up early ready to go.

I grabbed my gear and was taken to a vehicle which was driven onto the tarmac on the airstrip. As I exited, I quickly realized I would be on a Boeing EA-18G Growler. It was a super high-tech version of the F-18 hornet which was the aircraft seen in the Top Gun movie. The Navy had used them for years now but the EA-18G was a horse of another color.

The Growler was an imposing piece of war equipment. It can fly at 50,000 feet and has a maximum speed of 1,960 km/h.

I knew, even with additional fuel, its range was limited to around 1,500 km so deduced I was being flown to Italy before heading home.

As I got suited up and donned my helmet, I was greeted by Captain Thorne whose call sign was Rosy. These naval aviators were a real bunch of odd ducks sometimes. He explained that his job was to get me to the airbase at Aviano, Italy. Thanks to NATO this base was often used by US forces. It was a major location for staging during Desert Storm. He smiled at me and said we weren't going to set any speed records, but we would be landing in Aviano in about an hour. Plenty quick for me.

I knew that Aviano was in the North of Italy reasonably close to Venice so I was hoping the rest of my trip would be commercial. I was told I would be contacted once at the base with further instructions.

The flight was quick, and the aircraft just reeked of power. It is known as an electronic warfare aircraft and is the most complex piece of equipment I have ever seen. My attention was constantly split between the skies around me and the controls and guts of this formidable weapon.

While naval pilots are trained at the US Navy Fighter Weapons School, known as Topgun, EA-18G crews are trained at a different school. It is called the Airborne Electronic Attack Weapons School but known as Havoc. Havoc is not an acronym. It is named that because havoc is exactly what these aircraft cause in a battle situation. It had all manner of electronic warfare capability, most of which I was not aware. Both schools are headquartered at Naval Air Station Fallon in Nevada.

In no time, literally, we rolled to a stop on the tarmac and when I climbed down, I was greeted by a Navy personnel who said simply, "Tom sent me to get you acclimated."

I said great and was directed to a waiting vehicle. He looked in the rear-view mirror as he said, "I was told you wanted to see Venice so that's where your hotel is." I thought that was a nice atta boy trip so relaxed and enjoyed the view.

I was really just destressing and trying to begin to relax as I would after any mission. Soon we pulled into a hotel called the Palazzo Veneziano which looked to be about a four-star hotel. It was close to the grand canal by the bridge which was the one copied in Las Vegas at the Venetian. I thanked the driver and checked in at the desk and was shown to my room.

Once the bellman was gone, I locked the door behind me and took in the view. There was a cell phone on the table and a note with directions and a number to call Tom in the morning. I was pleased to see the room was well appointed including a large soaker tub. I drew a hot bath, stripped, and slid into the almost scalding water after securing a bottle of wine and a glass.

I relaxed the best I knew how and planned a few of the sights I wanted to see. Hopefully, I would be allowed time to do so.

Chapter 20 Nine – Just Another Tourist

As instructed, I called SECNAV at the designated time and was pleased to hear Tom's voice. He congratulated me on yet another successful mission and asked how much time I wanted in Italy before coming home. I said that a week would likely be just right. He told me to look in the safe in the room advising the combination was our out-date from the Teams. He said that everything I needed was in there, including an open-ended ticket home.

We chatted for a minute or two more and then I hung up and went to the safe. There was my own passport, Driver's License, and a platinum AMEX in my name. THIS would be a lot of fun.

I spent the next hour meticulously planning what I would do for the next five or six days. The Amalfi Coast, the Vatican, the Colosseum, and a wine tasting experience in the Tuscan countryside. Thanks to Kathy, Jonathon, Angela, and Luke my taste in wines was really coming along. All the cash he had made for me on my investments didn't hurt either. I took a minute to contemplate why I felt like I had to continue working when I had more than enough money to live very comfortably for the rest of my days.

I finally arrived at the conclusion that I needed to help people, I needed to right the wrongs that were happening, wherever that led me. I suppose that was why Tom knew I would be a willing participant in his plan.

By day five I knew I was close to the end of my tour. While I, of course, enjoyed seeing all the sights I had been anticipating the winery tour and tasting in Tuscany. I was already eager to regale Jonathon with tales of each winery and the vintages I was about to sample.

The tour was simply amazing. There were only three others with me. An older couple who I would find out were retired government workers living off their pensions and investments and a younger fellow who did something in IT. They all reeked of wealth, so I felt a bit out of place but was never made to feel that way. We all got along fabulously.

As we rolled through the hillsides I marvelled at the sheer volume of wineries and vines that absolutely filled the countryside. It seemed everything was either grapes or olives in the whole region. The wineries we would be visiting included two in the Chianti Classico region and one Brunello specialty winery.

The Brunello was my favorite. As we rolled though the gates, I was amazed at the almost purple color of the Sangiovese grapes from which Brunello do Montalcino is made. It is a full bodied, elegant red that I was eager to experience here at ground zero. I found the tour truly fascinating and could not wait to return home and share the experience with my friends.

The tastes, sights and sounds of that tour occupied my mind almost the whole flight home. I still have to admit, I was very happy to land back at LAX and make my way to my house.

As we motored down the coast, I began to wonder what Thomas might have in mind for me next. Would I be rescuing another kidnapped child? It was always difficult for me to turn my mind off and simply enjoy my surroundings, but I really was making an effort to improve.

Finally, we arrived at my house. I thanked the driver and kicked off my shoes as I walked through the door. I slept on and off for the next couple of days after my fifteen-hour flight and took my time getting back in touch with everyone. I got a little antsy the third day and phoned Norie, Kathy, Angela and even Colin.

As far as they all knew I had simply returned from a vacation, and I did my best to make it seem so. It took about two weeks for Tom to get back in touch with me, asking me if we could meet at my favorite restaurant. I immediately wondered why he wouldn't simply mention Duke's by name but went with it anyway.

Chapter Thirty – Back In The Saddle, AGAIN

I was pleased to meet Tom at Duke's as it was yet another in a very long line of perfect California days at the beach. I was really anxious to go surfing but when the Secretary of the Navy contacts you there isn't an option to delay.

He dove right into things after thanking me for what I had just done. He asked what I knew about the Somali pirate situation. I explained that I only knew what was reported and he began to go into detail about what was NOT being reported. Since the early 90's when the Somali Civil War seemed to give birth to a full-scale pirate movement many ships had been assaulted and/or captured for ransom.

A task force known as the Combined Task Force 150 was established in the Gulf of Aden to combat these thieves and terrorists. It involved 33 nations and they made decent headway, but it was being noticed there were many repeat offenders. Tom said that he had been directed to take more aggressive action, in an off-the-books style.

He explained that simply arresting these people was not sending the right message. Water cannons and capture were not eliminating the problem.

That was when he advised there were other SEALS, like me, who had left the Teams but still itched to protect the world. I smiled when he included Sonny and Travis in that short list.

He went on to explain there were eight of us willing to "go back to work."

I had heard of most of them and worked with four of them previously, including Sonny and Travis. He said that if I agreed this would be the last time we would speak. The group would meet privately and have access to all sorts of classified and regular weaponry and surveillance equipment. I was given an address of a house in Huntington Beach as well as a date and time.

The cover story for any inquisitive neighbors was handled by our live-in domestic and her husband. When I attended our first get together, I chuckled at the racial makeup of our group. Clearly, SECNAV had chosen this group to fit in with multiple vessels that travelled that area. There was nothing clearly obvious that this was a group of Americans. Myself, a couple of Italian guys, two who looked Mediterranean and three others, including another female, who were black.

Even sitting there in casual clothes, it was clear that this was team like no other. We spent that first meeting discussing our strengths and whether or not there were any weaknesses. There were very few of those.

I immediately felt safe and comfortable working this group and having Sonny and Travis really helped too.

It was a week later when we were asked to meet at the house again. All of us piled into a van with blacked out windows that looked like a plumbing van so we could drive straight into the garage without being seen. There were few words said as we all piled into the back at a parking lot miles away and out of sight.

When we arrived, there was already a man waiting. He looked like an insurance salesman but there was where it ended. He passed us each a package of information and then began to talk about the problems with these Somali pirates.

Standard justice was simply not working. There needed to be a different approach, but the US could not be perceived as being involved. Most everything we were about to do would happen in secrecy and silence. As SEALS we were all quite used to that so it wouldn't be difficult.

One of the issues with the current situation was that, once engaged, the pirates would quickly speed off to Somali territorial waters so the chase would often end there.

The Gulf of Aden is a relatively narrow corridor between the Arabian Sea and the Red Sea bordered on the North by Yemen and the South my Ethiopia, Eritrea, and Somalia. It was a very difficult place in which to operate, and even more difficult to operate completely under the radar.

The closest US airbase was actually Northeast of Saudi Arabia in Qatar. Most people pronounce it Ka-Tar, but it is actually pronounced "cutter" and it just drives me crazy when people don't say it properly. There is a US naval base called Camp Lemonnier closer and it is situated next to Djibouti.

There is a US air base right in Somalia, but its activity is drone-focussed. There is even a private US contractor there training Somali army commandos. That would likely be off limits to us anyway due to the secrecy requirement.

It would turn out that multiple locations would be used for weapons drops and tactical backup for us. It was made clear to us that ANY direct contact with US forces would be as an absolute last resort. We would plan out missions based on each situation and decide amongst ourselves how best to take these people out.

Our goal was simple, to eliminate as many of these pirates as possible.

We had multiple heated discussions and finally agreed that we would see if a "public hanging" would slow down their efforts. We would take a group of pirates as close to the gulf as possible. Once we had them, we would execute them in as grisly a manner as possible and ensure the boat or boats got back to a known harbor for these pirates.

We thought it to be a good first step. These pirates had basic armaments; they were typically enough to get past water cannons on commercial ships though. We would wait on the shore, hidden until we were advised that pirates had hit a ship. Once that was communicated, we would move out to their location on an intercept between them and the Somali coast.

It would require us to take up a secret position, most likely in Yemen and in the worst case, the Somali coast to wait. There was no way that we could be physically on the ships as the danger of us being discovered was too great.

We left one week later and soon found ourselves making our way to Djibouti. Once there we were given quarters in a secluded area of Camp Lemonnier. I quickly got the impression they were used to, and comfortable, with private citizens and secrecy. I mean, I don't think many US citizens, or even politicians know the depth of operations we handle outside of our continent. Since 9/11 our vigilance has increased all around the world and our secrecy has been in lockstep with it.

We were completely left to our own devices but had free run of the whole base. The command was told that we were a private contractor doing mostly oceanographic work. We did have one on-base contact who advised us where our equipment could be found and how to access it.

The first time we made a foray to see what we had I busted a gut. I knew why they wanted SEALS now. The only way to approach the locations was via the water. It was a hidden cave that opened up onto some land back against the rocks. I looked at the others as we stood up next to the boats and said, "This joint looks like the damn bat-cave." Jen laughed first and added, "but WAY better equipped."

We all got out of our gear and began to assess what was there. All manner of automatic weapons, RPGs, and other armament along with ammo was in weather-sealed lockers and tubs along the back wall. There were two high-power rigid inflatables as well as a mini sub and a few underwater diver propulsion units.

There was a full suite of dry suits and typical SEAL gear although there were no markings anywhere.

We went over the RIB's and noted they had significant monitoring capability and loads of power. The motors were the quietest one could get, with each craft holding three Honda outboards sticking out into the depths.

Once we fired one up it was clear that additional work had been done to these. I had never been so close to this much horsepower that was this quiet.

We each went in teams of two to evaluate and assess all the electronics in each boat. With their low profile and quietness, they would be extremely difficult to spot in the open sea, even during daylight hours. We gathered together around the table that had been setup and discussed our next steps.

Each team of two would take a three-hour shift monitoring the radios and satellite imaging of the area. One of the laptops was connected to a larger screen that displayed all the ship movements in the area along with their schedules and cargo. These pirates had taken oil tankers and container ships for ransom but had also captured larger private yachts where they could extract similar ransom amounts. We had to watch everything.

It would be tedious work with many hours filled with little activity. Jen and I said we would take first watch. We took the opportunity to talk about our past and she was impressed when she discovered I had been a SEAL. Turned out she was a former senior intelligence officer who had acquired a great deal of combat skills.

She was the only non-SEAL in our group, which gave me a little cause for concern. To be honest, I was shocked she was included but I would later discover she most surely COULD have been a SEAL.

Chapter Thirty 1 – Pirates Ahoy

We waited patiently for days, occupying ourselves with various training activities to stay sharp and equal amounts of rest time to ensure we remained in top form. Just when we were all starting to get a little itchy something finally broke.

Travis called us all over and we watched a ship stopping in the Gulf. He switched us to satellite overwatch and it was clear there were pirates. They had surrounded the ship with four smaller craft, and we watched as four of them made their way across the decks towards the pilothouse.

He kept watching as the rest of us geared up and got everything into the two boats. Night had fallen about two hours prior, so we would be able to get in and out without too much trouble. At least, that was our hope. Within thirty minutes seven of us were exiting the cave on two boats. Jen stayed behind to provide tactical support and overwatch to ensure we were not in any danger than absolutely necessary to fulfill our mission.

It took only thirty minutes for us to get close enough to the ship. The floodlights on the larger ship rendered our night-vision goggles useless as they were simply too bright. That was fine by us, we had all operated in much worse conditions against much better trained adversaries. These guys would have no idea what was about to hit them.

We could see all four boats now tied up to the ship and there was nothing to indicate any of them had stayed behind. With four boats we estimated as many sixteen attackers now on the ship. We would prefer to take each one down with non-lethal tactics and then get them into their own boats. Once there, it would be a shock and awe scenario where we would create as much blood and gore as possible.

Mercenaries like Somali pirates wanted cash, they didn't want to die. Once each craft was filled with nasty looking bodies, we would guide the boats as close to one of the Somali docks as we safely could and then move away before they were discovered.

We went to each side of the bow of the ship as once our boats were tied up to the ship, they would be invisible from the deck. We coordinated our climbs up each side and waited at the lip of the deck. There were two of us on each side of the bow waiting on the ropes. Our earpieces crackled with Jen telling us the bow was now open, there were no pirates within view of the prow of the ship.

The four of us quickly scrambled up and hid behind the superstructure. The other three were in the water swimming cautiously toward the pirate boats. Each of us was prepared, Ka-Bar knife in hand, and ready for action.

The butt of the knife was great for knocking someone out cold and that would be the first choice. That or a strike and choke hold so that the pirate boats would be filled with bloody corpses when they were eventually spotted.

We moved slowly and silently up the ship and we finally spotted two pirates. Luckily, they weren't sophisticated enough to be using radios. They likely checked in with flashlights or lighters if they checked in at all.

I nodded to Sonny to take the one on the right and I would take the one on the left. We moved towards them and while I chose to choke mine out, Sonny drove the butt of his knife into the back of his guy's skull. Either way, they were both unconscious in seconds. We stashed both bodies, after a quick twist snapped their necks, against the bulkhead of the crew quarters.

We left Travis behind to monitor them in case they were discovered. The six of us then moved quickly forward in teams of two to disable the rest of the pirates. We spotted the crew locked up in the mess, which had an outside viewing porthole. It appeared for a ship of this type; the whole crew were all being held in that room. It would likely be only the captain and a navigator who might still be on the bridge. That would help.

We split up and began our search. Every few minutes our earpieces would crackle with one of us saying simply, "one more down."

We knew Jen was keeping track of numbers, but we were also each counting too. Force of habit I suppose.

As we took out each one, we drug them down the deck to the closest possible hiding place and left the bodies for later. It was another eight or so minutes before we heard Jen advise there were only expected to be two left and they were both in the wheelhouse. Sonny and I went up one side while Gordo and Gianni went up the other. It was completely dark outside, and we were able to get glances inside of who was where.

Their guard was down, and they were looking somewhat relaxed.

Clearly the Captain had been pistol-whipped and the other crew guy looked like he had taken a few punches. The pirates didn't feel they were at any risk at the moment.

It was a warm night and both hatches were open. They had no idea that the cross breeze they were currently enjoying would soon be their downfall. With the hostages, it was too dangerous for us to attempt a takedown without guns, but we decided to wait a few minutes.

The ship was rolling lazily on the seas as large ships do. It was a calm night so shooting them would have been relatively easy, at least for us. Then we caught a break.

The guy guarding the captain put his gun into his belt and moved toward the door. The other guy was focussed on him, and the captain and he was close enough to the door for Sonny to take him.

As the pirate got closer and closer to my hatch, I heard Sonny counting down in my ear, 3, 2, 1, NOW. I grabbed him by the neck and spun him outside and was surprised that he had some fighting skills. His gun had fallen out, but he reached into the back of his belt to pull out a large knife. I grabbed my Ka-Bar from my belt, and we squared off.

He swung wildly at me as I easily deflected his blade using my own. I really didn't feel like letting this go too far so the next time he lunged a put a deep slice into his forearm. When the knife fell from his hand I closed quickly and delivered a hard elbow right onto the end of his jaw.

He went down like a Georges St. Pierre opponent. GSP as they call him, is a famous Canadian MMA guy and one of my favorites. I zip tied him quickly and then looked to Sonny. He just smiled and said, "what took so long?"

It took us a while, but we lowered all the bodies down, spreading them around into all four boats. We then hooked two up to each of our RIB's and began motoring towards Somalia.

Thanks to the satellite history Jen was able to give us a close approximation of the area from which they departed on their mission.

We arrived in about thirty minutes and one of us got into each boat. One by one the pirates were cut and slashed. Grisly stuff that would never been sanctioned by the US military in any way. Tongues were cut out, throats slashed, and deep knife wounds made across their faces. We needed whoever found them to think each was tortured and died a horrific death.

The hope was this would be the deterrent needed. Trials weren't working and the Somali government seemed to condone more or less what was happening since their fishery had all but dried up. I supposed that we would soon see. It would take a while for word to spread.

We pointed the boats towards the coordinates Jen had given us and set each motor to a little past idle. We watched as they headed toward their destination and then returned quickly to our cave. There was no way we wanted to be caught in open water once those guys were discovered. As we motored back, Jen kept us apprised of their progress.

We were back in our cave with boats safely moored and already refueled long before the pirate boats hit the shore of Somalia.

We relaxed around a fire as we rehashed the mission, including what we could have done differently.

Clearly this cave was setup with direct input from SECNAV. There was a quiet, large scale generator providing power with many of the amenities of home, including a fully stocked beer fridge or two. It was quite the setup and I wondered how they were able to accomplish this.

I would later find out that the government in Djibouti was tiring of the bad karma that these pirates were bringing to their area. Being neighbors with Somalia was no walk in the park. They were quite helpful in getting this area setup and keeping it off everyone's radar. I would come to appreciate Tom telling me that in confidence and it spoke to the trust he had in me. No different than when were operating together.

We left only one sentry monitoring everything while we all dozed off to sleep. I enjoyed the sounds of the waves gently rolling into our little cove and then softly breaking on the sand at the front of our cave. It was so relaxing and with the fire now out we had opened the blackout blind that hid us so we could see out to the open ocean and the stars.

Other than the fact we were there to kill and maim people this would have been one heck of a vacation, at least for a SEAL.

As I drifted off, I again realized how much I missed this camaraderie, the shared commitment to one another and the mission. It gave me purpose and I wondered if I could ever truly "retire."

I supposed at some point, my body would betray me, but I knew that was a long way off. In many ways I was at the top of my game, and perhaps even better.

Chapter Thirty 2 – We're Yachties Now

After our first outing it remained surprisingly quiet. I suppose we were not expecting to see anything much on the news but there should have been something! Jen was able to confirm that all four craft indeed hit shore and two of the four were in an area know to be Pirate-friendly.

We remained on high alert as we waited for the other shoe to drop. We monitored all channels and oversight 24 hours a day. It was the fourth day when we heard a distress call from a yacht. Luckily, the pirates didn't have the power to catch this one. It was smaller than a super yacht and it had tons of power. They simply outran the would-be thieves.

That was when we had the idea. Three of us almost simultaneously said, "why don't we use a bait boat?" We began to discuss how LA and other city police forces had successfully used bait cars to trap and prosecute criminals. Of course, we didn't really want to trap anyone.

We broached the idea that we should get a superyacht and motor around international waters. At some point in time pirates would approach us and rather than capture them or anything else we would blow all evidence of them to kingdom come. It seemed such a simple idea and even somewhat elegant to us all. We drafted a plan and had it run up the flagpole.

I think we were all somewhat shocked when we were given the go ahead. We were told there would be a 180-foot superyacht waiting for us in the next two weeks. It actually took three weeks before we were notified where and when the yacht would pick us up. Jen would take us out to the coordinates that would be provided and then return to our cave to monitor everything.

The following day we all awoke early and began to prepare all our gear and weaponry. We were advised the boat would have three RPG launchers along with a good supply of ordnance. We would need to ensure that anything we did remained unseen. Fortunately, the pirates were smart enough not to attack ships when there were others close by who could potentially offer assistance, they counted on remoteness.

Little did they know that this need to operate in secrecy and isolation would soon lead to their demise. We were operating in international waters, and we were well aware what we were doing was clearly in violation of maritime law. But the law had not done such an excellent job of eliminating the pirate problem. We were all comfortable with being judge, jury and executioner so had no qualms with blowing these criminals up.

We motored up on the yacht and, even for a sailor, it was an impressive unit. It looked even longer than expected and very, very sleek.

It appeared to have at least four decks. The Ali Hassan was a real work of art and would certainly attract interest from pirates looking to capture wealthy ransom victims. Although it had a broad beam the prow of the ship narrowed to an almost razor-like edge giving it excellent ability to cut smoothly through the seas.

Of course, we would have no need to run from anyone but could make some good miles if required. Sometimes you might need to outrun a storm that surfaced too quickly to be given much notice.

We were all boarded and introduced to the captain and crew, all of whom knew what we were going to be doing. They were being paid well and secrecy wasn't a worry as most all had prior experience with pirates and were supportive of eradicating the problem.

We all sat around a large dining table that would be our main planning area. We highlighted on maps two primary areas where we believed we should focus due to previous activity. Often these pirates would strike as ships approached the gulf of Aden. They seemed to be launching from somewhere near Bosaso, which was right on the gulf. The other main area straight out from the coast into the Indian Ocean North of Mogadishu. The best intel to date put them close to Hobyo, which is up the coast about 190 km from Mogadishu.

It wouldn't matter where they came from, they would be unable to hide and definitely unable to run once we spotted them. Jen was monitoring the areas very closely as we motored slowly North. In addition to satellite coverage and radar, she had positioned all the movement of large commercial vessels including container ships and tankers which are both favorite targets of these pirates.

Any other pleasure yachts and other craft were all highlighted as well. Now it was a matter of us waiting for someone to try something.

Chapter Thirty 3 – The Attack Yacht

It only took two days for the first attempt to be made. Jen notified us that there were three boats making fairly good speed and on an intercept course. Clearly, these guys had spies on one or more commercial ships or other boats. It was unlikely they just motored around out here aimlessly looking for targets.

The seas weren't overly smooth as dusk approached but to a yacht this size that wouldn't really matter. We decided we would need to confirm the presence of weapons on board, and we would need to let at least one try to take us. That way we could be comfortable they were indeed pirates and could neutralize them with a clear conscience.

We had a fairly powerful radio signal blocker on board so even if they had phones or radios, once we turned the unit on all communication would cease. We positioned three of us, each with an RPG launcher at tactical locations so that we could cover all sides of the yacht. It had a large swim platform at the stern which would make it easy for them to attempt to board.

When they attacked larger ships, they were typically climbing up ropes or rope ladders so they would see this yacht as a simple deal. It would be the last thing they would see.

We waited and watched as the boats got closer and closer. They clearly believed they were going to have an easy time of this as they sent only two men onto the swim platform.

We watched as two of them climbed onto the platform and readied their guns. They both stepped into view at the same time, and both were neutralized with a single, sound suppressed, shot to the head. Just a pop sound and then a splash. Once Jen advised there were no other craft close enough to see anything we lit up all the boats simultaneously and fired RPGs dead center.

We wanted to sink them but ensure we didn't blow up any fuel tanks if we could avoid it. Once the grenades had done their work, we turned on all the floodlights around the boat and used our rifles to pick off any stragglers who survived the blast. It was all over in less than two minutes.

The boats were destroyed and sinking to the bottom of the sea and the bodies of the men were either sinking or about to be eaten by opportunistic feeders. We cleaned up the rear of the boat and stashed all our gear after preparing for the next attack. It was like a vacation for us compared to when we were SEALs.

We spent most of the days splashing around in the water and getting in some training. The yacht had a well-equipped weight room, and the ocean was our playground as far as swimming went. The pirates usually attacked at or very soon after dusk, counting on the light conditions to obscure their approach.

Their boats were small enough that radar might show them as whales, sharks or simply debris.

We stayed out there, splitting our time between the two regions, for almost a month. We dealt with four more groups of pirates, all of whom met their maker within minutes of first contact with us.

We kept the operation the same and the pirates obliged by using the swim platform on every attempted attack. It was almost too easy, and we wondered why we were the ones tasked with doing this. We would later find out that the secrecy was paramount, and SEALs were the only people SECNAV trusted with the task.

After that fifth group of pirates were dispatched, we were all ready to be done. This was well below our level of training and experience.

While it was nice to be needed and paid handsomely, it just felt beneath us to be turned into little more than assassins. Besides, things were starting to get a little tense.

There was chatter that even the government was wondering what was happening to all the pirates. Patrols were getting more frequent, and we were beginning to worry about getting caught. Our "bait boat" trick had likely reached the end of its useful life. Time to close up shop and move on.

It was great working with Sonny and Travis again and meeting the rest of the team, but I was more than ready to be back home. It was clear that everyone else shared my feelings when we parted company at the airbase after flying in from Djibouti.

Chapter Thirty 4 – Back Home Amongst Friends

I had been back home for a couple of days and began to contact friends. I called Colin first and he said that Kathy and Jonathon were having a party on Saturday, and I could go as his "date" to surprise everyone. I stopped phoning anyone else to preserve the surprise. They had all been asking about me, so I thought this was a great idea. Plus, I was really ready to catch a few waves!

Colin still lived just up the beach from the four amigos so we could just stroll down there. He said everything was getting started with some surfing around 1:00 PM, providing the weather and surf report held up, so that was what I planned. I couldn't wait for Saturday as I hadn't seen everyone together in quite a while. I had already decided to lay low for a month, so I contacted Tom Harker and said I needed a break. I was ready.

I was up early when Saturday arrived and went for a run to clear my head. It was a beautiful, sunny Southern California day AGAIN. I had checked the surf report and it was looking good, so I was pumped to get out with boys and grab some waves. I grabbed a shower, threw on some casual clothes, and hopped in the car. I turned into Colin's driveway at 12:30 and he came running out and gave me a big hug. It was always great to see Colin. I consider him one of my best friends forever.

I grabbed my bag, he grabbed his, and we strolled down the sand leisurely towards Jonathon's place. It felt great to feel the silky white sand under my feet and have the brilliant California sun warming my whole body. I could never imagine myself living anywhere else.

We could hear people partying already as we approached the house. I heard a loud scream when we turned the corner and Kathy came running up and gave me a bear-hug, almost knocking me over in the process. As she dragged me towards the house more and people came up to say hello. Of course, Jonathon was next, followed by Angela and Luke, Norie and a bunch of others including Arlo and Sage.

We were getting ribbed about being overdressed as everyone was in a bathing suit of some description. We went in to change and I came outside with my rash guard already on. Jonathon smiled and handed me my favorite board and we ran out into the surf. Jonathon, Luke, Colin, and me, were soon paddling through the waves on our way to our first rides of the day.

It was a perfect afternoon. Four-to-six-foot waves rolling in, set after set. We were spread out soon and watching the open ocean when the first opportunity came in. We had spaced ourselves far enough apart that two or three of us could ride the same wave. I caught the first one and left everyone behind.

I wore a broad smile as I cut back and forth across the face of the wave, easily moving up to the crest and sliding back down multiple times. I felt the cool saltwater mist splashing onto my face as I rode my first wave in months for all it was worth. Normally I would have turned out long before the wave died, but I didn't want this first one to end. I was going to go as far as possible.

When I finally jumped off my board, I was standing in only three feet of water and quickly turned, hopped over a couple of breakers, and began to paddle like mad. I wanted more and I wanted more NOW.

When I made it back out to the group everyone said it looked like I hadn't lost a step. I told them Dukie was a great surf coach and then began scanning for my next ride. We all surfed for about two hours and finally decided to paddle in when Jonathon said he needed a snack. I recalled I hadn't eaten since breakfast either and immediately realized, I too was famished.

We all rode a last wave and strode up the sand, placing all the boards into the racks Jonathon had in his private surf-hut. We grabbed a seat along with the group and began to dig into the snacks spread across the table.

These guys were the hosts I always wanted to be, they thought of everything. I suppose they had a lot of experience and both Jonathon and Luke had been wealthy for quite a long while, so the girls were laser-focussed on entertaining.

I sat next to Norie, and we talked nonstop for at least an hour before we took a break. I really liked her. I thanked her again for hooking me up with Alexis Stone and said how helpful she had been.

Each time I got back with these folks , caught a few waves, and partied in the California sun I wondered why I wanted to be still working. What was wrong with me? But then, an opportunity would pop up and I knew exactly why I couldn't just surf all day and goof off.

Deep down, I wanted to help people. I wanted to stop criminals in their tracks and, if I'm being honest, I really enjoyed kicking the crap out of someone who deserved it. There was no doubt ever that I was a 50/ 50 blend of my parents. They had both dedicated their lives to helping others and enforcing the law. They would not be completely pleased about how I was getting some things done but overall, I think they would be proud.

The very next thought if my head was what was next? Geez, I hadn't even finished enjoying my first relaxing party in a long while and I was already wondering what Tom would have me doing next.

Chapter Thirty 5 – Me Time

The party was great but really got me relaxing was getting back to training. Running, MMA and some weapons work always made me feel like me. I prided myself on always staying sharp, but I also knew SECNAV would need me at full speed when he next called.

Each day I would rise at precisely 07:00 and start with some light stretching in preparation for a beach run. By 07:20 I was out of the house and striding down the beach. Each day I alternated my distance and intensity to ensure I was getting the most bang for my exercise buck. I simply loved running along the beach as the sand began to warm. I was easily mesmerized as my steps were like the pounding of a drum to the cadence of the songs playing on my earbuds.

It was almost a trancelike state for me with my whole body in synch to the music, heart pounding gently in my chest even during full out sprints. I had really come to appreciate both the physical and mental benefits of a challenging run. In some ways, it was the equal to a great sparring session.

I turned for home after getting in a comfortable three miles and began to pick up my pace each ¼ mile heading home. Each segment quicker than the last, more insistent, focussed on the pace and length of my stride. I always made it a policy to run the penultimate half mile at almost full speed. After putting in four, five or six miles already doing a final half mile all out was how you really made gains in both speed and endurance.

There were now people starting to lay out on the beach, but they were blurs as I blazed past them. Finally, my watch alerted me there was a half mile to go and I dialed it back to comfortable, cool down pace. The sun was moving higher into the sky and the temperature had already gone up by at least 15 degrees during my run. It would be a good afternoon to be in a climate-controlled gym honing my attack and defense skills.

I had met an excellent training partner only a few months back. For me, it was a real challenge to find men who were willing to train with and spar with a woman, who in many cases could kick their ass. This guy wasn't encumbered by any such fears. His name was George, with an "S" at the end. I would learn that he was a French-Canadian guy and a very accomplished MMA fighter.

Georges St. Pierre, or GSP as his friends often refer to him, is a real machine. He gave up competing a couple of years ago but fought in the Welterweight and Middleweight divisions. His typical weight is 170 so he was good match for me size-wise. At the age of only 12 he had received his 2nd dan Kyokushin karate black belt. He changed to MMA when his coach died, Georges was only 16.

Georges was really a great guy and if you saw him in street clothes there was nothing to indicate that he could tear most people apart. I quickly began to enjoy training with him. He had given up weight training and moved to more gymnastics style training using parallel bars, rings, pommel horse and other gymnastics equipment.

Like me, he had done his fair share of weight training and had huge powerful legs. He realized that gymnastics, stretching and working on flexibility would further extend his career. Plus, it was easier on the body! He only lived here about half the year as he would return to Montreal, where he was born, each summer and fall.

He was really an all-around nice guy and we hit it off immediately. Our sparring was more technical than anything as I don't think going all-out would be good for either one of us. The other benefit of not going 100% is it would allow both of us to maintain our fighting egos. Never a bad thing. The other benefit was we were unequivocally just friends. There was never a worry about either one of us doing something silly like attempting a date. With us, it was just two fighters training.

I did invite him to a party once and he seemed to have a really fun time. Nobody recognized him, which he really liked. He enjoyed being just one of the guys, although in swim trunks he clearly wasn't JUST one of the guys.

He was an amazing physical specimen and kept himself in top shape. I think that was why we enjoyed training together almost as soon as we first met. We both had the same goal, to be in top shape all the time.

There was a huge responsibility to being like Georges or myself. We knew how easy it could be for us to be lethal. Me much more than him I suppose, but we still discussed how we must react if ever confronted.

It was odd then that only the day after we had that conversation I was faced with an exceedingly difficult decision. I was in a parking lot and heard a bit of a commotion a few cars away. When I looked over there were two menacing looking dudes screaming at an older gentleman. I walked their direction and saw the most minor of scrapes on what I assumed was their car. Apparently, the gentleman had started to back out of his stall and bumped into their car.

I walked up and asked if he was okay and one of the guys scowled at me and said, "it's none of your business bitch. Stay out of it." He was a greasy looking, biker type guy. Longer, messy hair, and the beginning of a beard. The other guy could have been his twin. Unfortunately, both were quite large so I knew they would not respond well to me intervening. However, when one of them got right up in the man's face, I asked, as politely as I could, for them to leave him alone.

That was all it took for that guy to focus his attention on me. "I thought I told you to mind your own business," he barked at me. I then did everything I could to warn them and try to get them to leave the guy alone. I said he was just an old guy, what were they going to do? Beat him up for a little bump on their car? He took a step closer to me and lifted the corner of his shirt, letting me catch a glimpse of the handle of a pistol. "You don't listen well, do you?"

As I replied with, "no I don't," I delivered a powerful kick to the inside of his knee. With his size I knew he would be unable to steady himself so on the way down I brought up a second kick catching him on the jaw as he fell. He was out cold. I figured the other one likely had a pistol as well, so I shoved the older man behind the vehicle as I moved quickly. I knew I had to prevent him from retrieving his pistol or at the very least prevent him from directing any shots at the man or me. As he reached behind his back, I dove straight at him guiding my arm between his own arm and his body.

As my body followed behind, I used the leverage to snap his arm around and that caused him to drop the pistol. Now I was mad, which was not going to be good for him. I let him square off in front of me and dodged him as he lunged towards me. I could have subdued him quite easily then, but I knew I wanted more. He came back around at me, and I hit him hard with a blow to the side of his head.

He tried to swing at me a few more times but I easily dodged his attempts. I had beaten men two or three times quicker than this idiot and he clearly had no training except for street fighting. I should have let it go but he was yapping again and calling me all sorts of names. I just smiled at him and asked what his mother would think if she heard him.

That seemed to make him even crazier and when he came at me this time, I delivered a strike right to his mouth that opened up a large cut. He was spitting blood and yelling at me at the same time. Out of the corner of my eye I spotted his partner trying to get up and as I stepped to the side, I gave him a spinning back kick that connected squarely with his head.

He was down and out again, and I decided it was time to be done with these bozos. I let him get a little closer and with three quick strikes I knew I had blown up one eye socket, blackened the other and knocked out a couple of teeth at least. They were both on the ground as the police rolled up, assessed the situation immediately put me in cuffs and got me into the back of a car. The other two were grabbed at the same time and put in separate cars.

When the officer finally began to ask questions, I was calm and concise in my answers. I explained they both had guns and told him to talk to the older gentleman who had waited around.

He turned around to face me and said, "Oh, we don't need to. We know these two very well." He smiled and added, "I'll deny it if this gets out, but you just performed a huge public service."

When all was said and done, I just went home and grabbed a shower. I chuckled when I remembered Georges and I discussing this very type of thing. Oh well. That was my problem when I was getting ready for any kind of mission. My sense of right and wrong was heightened and my aggressiveness began to ramp up along with it. It was not the best combination for me, or anyone around me with evil tendencies.

Soon, I was entering my fourth week at home, and I just had a feeling I was about to hear from Tom. I was aware there were significant exercises going on at Coronado so it was quite likely he would be there. I knew I was on the money with my sense when I received an invite to Coronado. I got a phone call from Travis the next day saying he had been "invited" as well so now I knew something was up.

Chapter Thirty 6 – Naval Amphibious Base Coronado

It was odd driving onto the base once again. Coronado was a great story. It was created in 1943 when the Navy had the San Diego Bay dredged to allow larger ships in WW2 to steam directly into San Diego. It houses over thirty different commands now and more acronyms than anyone would ever want to learn. I may be biased, but the most notable command there are the Navy SEAL Teams based on the West Coast.

Coronado provides an ideal training ground for SEALs thanks to 5,500 yards of Pacific Ocean and Bayfront beaches. There are a couple of species of birds there that are now on the endangered list, so the Navy lost about 40% of the beach area to nesting. The Navy even patrols the beaches to seek out predators of the Western Snowy Plover and the California Least Tern, whatever the heck they are. That still left loads of beachfront on which to train and hone the skills of the world's deadliest fighting force.

Things had really changed since I left the Teams. Who would have thought a couple of birds would displace one of the most famous tactical groups on the planet? I guess that's the direction the world is going. I'm all for saving endangered species but I think there might be some limits.

Anyway, the guard checked my ID against his list while his partner scanned and checked my vehicle. I was directed to building S-8 and given a map. I didn't need the map. I knew exactly where I was headed. Minutes later I stepped through the door into a private briefing room and was greeted by Travis and Sonny. They introduced me to a few other guys, and we all sat down.

The door opened and SECNAV stepped through looking very businesslike.

He welcomed everyone and thanked us all for coming. He looked at Sonny, Travis and I and thanked us directly for getting the job done. He said things have really calmed down in the region. That was it. Everything SEALs ever did was on a need-to-know basis and that would not change here.

His aide left the room, and the doors were locked. Tom looked around the room and began to speak. He advised that everything discussed today and happening with this team was, as usual, absolute top secret. There would be nobody other than his designated contact who would speak with us from here on out. What we were about to do was paramount to the safety of the United States and most of the rest of the world. He then asked us to stand to confirm we were in. All of us stood up and looked at each other and then sat back down when he said, "okay then, let's get going."

He said there was intel that had recently surfaced around Kim Jong Un and his future plans.

Since he became the leader of North Korea, it was immediately apparent he is a whack-job. He had members of his own family assassinated and has pushed the country to expand its nuclear armaments and delivery systems for those catastrophic weapons. Tom explained that China even has concerns about him and that says a lot. China doesn't exactly play nice with the USA and honest communication has never been a priority for either side. It was discovered that Kim Jong Un was planning a trip to Vietnam, one of the few times he would leave his country to go somewhere other than China.

It was determined by cake-eaters well above our pay grade that this would be a prime opportunity for him to have a horrific "accident." This team was going to orchestrate that event. It could not be in any way, shape or form viewed as an assassination by the US, at least a provable one. There could be no guns or knives or anything of the sort.

We had been informed that we could base the operation in Subic Bay in the Philippines. It was on the island of Luzon which was about 50 miles from Manilla. One of the advantages of this location is that it lies directly across from Vietnam via the South China Sea. We all felt comfortable that we could get in and out without being detected although we would much rather have the opportunity elsewhere. Operating in such close proximity to China made the mission extremely dangerous.

This would be our best opportunity so we began many discussions of exactly how we might accomplish this with as little collateral damage as possible. We were not about to become terrorists at this point in our lives.

Chapter Thirty 7 – Secret Weapons

The United States is always the first to call out other countries on things like nuclear proliferation, missile tests and such but we maintain our own test and development sites. At any given time, the US has scientists and generals working on multiple methods of disabling enemies and eliminating threats against the US.

It has really ramped back up since 9/11. Whether there were WMD or not doesn't matter. What matters is the hawks in the military are now listened to much more closely than ever before, even by the Democrats. The Joint Chiefs have never really changed. They espouse war supposedly to stop war. A scary concept.

We all well understood the danger that North Korea posed. To watch the things Kim does is, frankly, terrifying. His shows of military strength, weapon creation and testing are unnerving. The tension in South Korea, on any given day, is palpable. His aggression and attitude towards Japan, is equally upsetting. I love Australia too, but I would hate to live so close to so much craziness.

However, this could not be personal. Our work could never be personal. I did contemplate the stark difference between this and hunting for Somali pirates.

I would rather be blowing those scumbags out of the water, but this also was a job that must be done.

The Philippines is a little more than 8,000 miles from US soil, about 16 hours on a commercial flight. Compared to the USA it might as well be on another planet. I sincerely hope we would fly commercial for once. 16 or 20 hours on a military cargo plane adapted to handle people is no walk in the park.

We were advised that the next day we would be briefed on a new delivery system that had recently been perfected by our scientists and weapons experts. That was all we were told. We were directed to be at building X-10, which was right against the harbor, at 06:00. We finished our day of discussions, trained for an hour and a half, and then hit the mess hall. Even though there were thousands of personnel at Coronado there was little interaction outside your own group. This made it easy for us to just be there and remain relatively un-noticed.

I slept well that night and was eager and ready to go at 05:00. Typical for me. As a female earlier in my career I had always felt the need to perform even better than ANY teammate. My training, accomplishments and past success had now gotten me into a much better place. I really was "one of the guys" and had been for a few years.

I now knew that there was nobody who wouldn't put their life in my hands, and I felt the same about my brothers.

We ate together and then strolled silently over to the building. We gathered in a briefing room attached to the larger warehouse style building. We were all surprised when the door opened and SECNAV showed up.

After saying we would have no further contact with him, we knew something was afoot. As he strode purposefully to the front of the room, we all quickly grabbed a seat. By the time he turned to face us we were seated and focussed on him. Some habits just never left you.

He surveyed the room and began by telling us that he would share a mission with any one of us. We really were the best of the best and we needed to prove that one more time.

He went on to explain that Kim Jong Un was rattling his sabre again in advance of his trip to Vietnam and the President had serious concerns. He had multiple intelligence briefings over the last week with half of them being off-the-books and focused on North Korea. Apparently, satellites had revealed a renewed focus on nuclear testing within North Korea. It was becoming even more critical that the "situation" be remedied.

Tom looked at the group and went on to tell us that the US had made tremendous progress on multiple underwater vessels. He said we were about to see the first underwater vehicle capable of moving multiple people across the sea floor vast distances. They had solved issues with pressure sickness, blood oxygen levels or anything else associated with being submerged for extended periods of time in a small craft.

He went on to explain that what we were about to see was basically a submarine that was undetectable, could stay submerged for months if needed and whose occupants would experience NO ill effects. THIS was the delivery method he was referring to.

While a couple of us thought it would be a method of delivering poison, none of us considered it would be a way to deliver US. We were then led into the adjoining area.

It looked like nothing any of us had ever seen. It was the submariner's version of a stealth bomber we were told. It was virtually undetectable and could travel at amazing speeds in open water. I could see the others were all having the same thoughts I was. There was no way anyone was travelling underwater for more than 1,000 kilometres and getting to Vietnam in time to get Kim.

This was the first time we were given any real details of what was happening.

Tom said that Kim would be in Hanoi, the capital, for two full days. What the US was also aware of was that Kim was planning a side trip to Phnom Penh, the capital of Cambodia. Very few people knew of this but thanks to our sophisticated monitoring of North Korea, we knew this to be the case. Getting in and out of Phnom Penh would be easier than Hanoi, although still extremely dangerous.

We would stage ourselves in Bangkok and would have multiple points of access and egress. Thanks to the growing tourism industry in Thailand, we would be able to fit in and would give ourselves the best chance of getting out of the region. That did not answer the many questions about getting IN, however.

Bangkok to Phnom Penh is about 700 kilometres by road and Phnom Penh is almost 3 hours from the coast. The safest water access point would likely be Sihanoukville. There are popular beaches there and direct access to water, an airport and a highway leading to Bangkok. I always preferred to have multiple routes and methods for exfil, so those facts gave me comfort.

We took a closer look at the craft and quickly got back to the task at hand. We were introduced to the operator, and he began to go into more detail. He said it was equipped with an air purification system that worked like the backpack rebreathers that had revolutionized SCUBA diving.

As such, it could stay submerged with no ill effects on its passengers for weeks at a time. Nuclear powered, and using a unique propulsion system, it operated as close to invisibly as anything could.

Tom said that we would use a delayed action poison that would stop Kim's heart and be undetectable once it did. It wouldn't show up on autopsy and the delay would give us more than 12 hours to make our escape. This would make using the highway to get to Bangkok a viable option. Once there we would just be a few more tourists.

Tom further laid out that they had built a complete and very thorough backstory on one of Kim's trusted advisors. He would be the one set up as the most likely party to have killed him. Thanks to CIA intelligence, Tom had been made aware that this particular individual often challenged Kim, at least as much as you can without getting yourself killed.

He was actually a cousin, and we also knew that he had been close to Jang Song Thaek, the uncle that Kim had executed.

Kim was under the impression that he was plotting to overthrow the government so had him executed. The dead body, with his own head sitting on his chest, was put on display. He was not a direct member of the Kim family but had married into it. Song-Thaek had married Kim Kyong-hui who was the only daughter of Kim Il-sung.

That made him an uncle by marriage of Kim Jong Un so trust would be hard for him to build with the notorious leader. Against the odds, he had built trust to a good level at this point and would be with Kim for the whole trip.

We met for a few hours afterward and Tom thanked us for our planning and discussion, but this was now to be the method we would use. The best option would still be for 2 or 3 of us to pose as tourists moving through Thailand and then work our way through Cambodia. The others were to provide overwatch and backup to ensure that, if anything happened, they could get us out.

He looked at me, Sonny and Travis and told us to get ready to be the most important tourists on this planet. I chuckled and said did it really seem plausible that I would be with either of these lunkheads? The room erupted in laughter but quicky settled.

We would all travel in the submersible and be dropped up the coast close to the Southern tip of Thailand. We would have vehicles there ready for us along with anything else we might need. The others would remain in Thailand, checking out beaches and tourist sites like the town of Chiang Mai and Phuket.

Thailand had become an extremely popular tourist area over the last 20 years or so and that made it completely plausible for the boys to hide in plain sight.

We wondered to ourselves why we didn't just arrive as tourists but agreed there must be good reason to enter one way and leave another. We knew there were always details left unsaid on almost every SEAL mission and we were not the types to question authority. We would be leaving the next morning at 06:00 so we should all eat, relax and rack early.

Chapter Thirty 8 – Tourist Time

05:00 hours seemed to arrive early, but I always had the same experience when we were getting spun up. We never talked about it, but we were all fairly similar in that way. We geared up, double checked all our "touristy" luggage, and got on the transport to take us to the airport for our flight to the Philippines.

We were flying into the Ninoy Aquino International Airport as it accepted direct flights from LA. I would have preferred Subic Bay which had opened when the Subic Bay naval base closed. I had assumed we would land at Ninoy Aquino International Airport as it was the closest to Luzon, but Subic Bay would require less overland travel. Landing at Ninoy Aquino would require us then to drive more than 2 ½ hours to get to Subic Bay.

There was another of the stealth submersibles waiting there for us, just off the coast. Each of us was given a complete set of papers including Philippine visas that were required. I was glad it was February as that would be the dry season. While the weather would still sit around 80 degrees Fahrenheit, at least it wouldn't be deadly humid.

We were let off at LAX in three separate groups. We were booked on a Philippine Airlines direct flight to Manila. It would be a 14 ½ hour flight leaving at 1:00 PM and arriving the next day at 6:25 PM local time.

I didn't relish sitting in a cramped, scum-class, seat so was thrilled when Travis mentioned that we were in business class.

We got all checked in and moved to our seats, which were those lay-flat ones that allow you to fully stretch out as if you were in a twin bed. We had all definitely slept in places MUCH worse than this! I was still shocked that we were booked business class.

Chapter Thirty 9 – Mission Aborted

We landed in Manila relatively well rested and were ready to get going. We were greeted by a driver who told us to throw our bags in the back and hop in as he had news for us.

Turned out he was a local operative. He told us he had been contacted by Tommy (our agreed upon codename for SECNAV) and told the mission had been scrubbed. We were all to return to Coronado immediately where we would be briefed.

We all sat wondering what the deal was while we were enroute back to the USA but ours had never been to question why.

Geez! 14 ½ hours to get to Manilla only to turn around a few hours after landing and head all the way back. We all nodded as we agreed that the cake-eaters were ruining things as usual.

Chapter 40 – New Direction

In what seemed like no time, some of us were back in the same room. Actually, some of us consisted of only Sonny, Travis, and me. It was Tom's aide who met with us this time, apologizing for the Tom's absence. That immediately got us all wondering. When plausible deniability seemed to be a requirement it always meant more danger for us.

He went to the front of the room and put a news bulletin on the screen. It dealt with the recent kidnapping of 15 American and one Canadian missionary in Haiti. It was the gang known as the 400 Mawozo who orchestrated the kidnapping. Usually, it was simply about money but this time they appeared to be serious when they threatened the lives of the 16 hostages in an attempt to extort the US of $16 million.

He said the President had now decided enough was enough. They couldn't pull off any strikes of course, and the Haitian police were inept at best and corrupt at worst. The US could not afford to be seen intervening in this Haitian issue so a small team would be the best approach. He looked at all three of us and said, "You are that team."

The problem in Haiti continues to worsen he went on the explain. 400 Mawozo is based in and around Port-au-Prince and their leader is Wilson Joseph.

They controlled roads and whole communities in and around the capital city. Haiti had a record number of kidnappings by various gangs in 2020 of 234. They had already passed 328 this year and it was only September! A real growth industry apparently.

They needed to be stopped. Getting rid of only Wilson Joseph would do no good, one of many other followers would simply step into his boots. The best approach would be to eliminate not just Joseph but the next thirty or forty in line. We were told that simply having these people killed would not be enough. They had to be brutally killed and either put on display or well published to the gangs what was going to happen to them.

The Haitian situation was interesting. The 400 Mawozo gang, whose name loosely translates to 400 idiots, started out as a petty crime gang. When the Haitian economy continued to slide backward, they elevated to kidnapping and collecting "tolls" on various public roads. The gang has been able to grow quickly, thanks in no small part to a lack of gun control in the country and corruption of public officials who benefit from gang activities such as high-profile ransom kidnappings.

The gang frequently holds its hostages and has gang activities in the Croix-des-Bouquets region.

It provides them ample cover and many places to hide due to its vastness and the fact there are hundreds of isolated hamlets throughout the region.

Although right next door to the idyllic beaches of the Dominican Republic the country of Haiti has always been a have-not country. It also lies in close proximity to Puerto Rico, so the United States has a personal stake in peace within the region. With Cuba sitting right across the Windward Passage of the Atlantic we would still need to be careful.

We went on to discuss that because Puerto Rico remains an unincorporated territory of the Unites States, we would be able to base ourselves there. The US acquired Puerto Rico after the Spanish-American war in 1898 and Puerto Ricans have been US citizens since 1917. This meant we could also travel freely between the mainland and Puerto Rico without arousing any suspicion.

Basing ourselves out of Guantanamo Bay in Cuba would add significant risk and challenge to any operation in the region. Cubans were not fans of the base and did not want Americans there. There was a naval base in Puerto Rico in Ceiba, which was closed down in 2004. It was called Roosevelt Roads and was known as a staging area for US ships and also using the island of Vieques as a target range for all types of ordnance.

Since the area had been vacated by the Navy it had, for the most part, been left untouched. The island of Vieques was off limits completely and nobody wanted to go there anyway.

That was why it made a perfect secret base for a couple of marine units and a temporary home for SEALs when they operated in the region. Isla de Vieques is located Southeast of the capital San Juan, off the opposite shore. It would provide easy access to Haiti or the Dominican via either the Caribbean Sea or Atlantic Ocean.

As discussion progressed, we agreed it would be less dangerous to get to Haiti via the Dominican Republic, once again just three tourists travelling around. We all looked the part with cameras around our necks, Tommy Bahama shirts on the guys, and sandals all around. I chuckled thinking we were definitely going to be the deadliest three tourists that region has ever seen.

We would fly into San Juan and take up residence there in a hotel close to the shoreline.

Chapter 40 One - Welcome to Puerto Rico

The San Juan Water and Beach Club Hotel was a lovely place. MUCH better than anywhere else we had been staged when we were active SEALs, to be sure. The rooms were large, and we had a suite with two bedrooms, connected via a locked door. It had a rooftop bar and even a rooftop pool that offered magnificent views all around. It was going to be a real shame to leave here so that we could stage everything at Vieques. Oh well.

We got settled in and our car was delivered along with watch size GPS devices, a number of knives and other weapons we requested. I had the pieces to make a few garrottes of course and there were multiple Ka-bar knives, a SEAL's favorite weapon. In addition, there were bags with the latest lightweight and thin bulletproof vests and all types of binoculars and night vision goggles. My two berretta's were there as well, equipped with suppressors and plenty of ammo.

It would be far too difficult to infiltrate any of the groups of the 400 Mawozo so we would operate in the background. Our plan was to lay a couple of traps initially and quickly turn the tables on the attempted kidnapping. Word would quickly spread and then we would move into darkness and start surprising them and eliminating them in a stealthier manner.

Operating within Port-Au-Prince would definitely be a challenge, but we did have a few things on our side. First, The Notre Dame de L'Assomption Cathedral had become a ruin back in 2010 courtesy of an earthquake. It had been abandoned and blockaded for years now.

We could easily gain access and use the various subterranean tunnels to move about freely. There was even a tunnel access to the Gulf of Gonave. Having direct water access was always comforting for a SEAL. There may be a few groups who might approach our level of work on land, but we all knew we had no equal when water was involved.

We headed out to Vieques in the morning to complete our preparations and get ready to head to the Dominican Republic, from which we would access Haiti. They had arranged a smaller super-yacht for us to travel on. The Dominican shoreline and beaches were tremendously popular with the wealthy types that frequented those yachts. Deep turquoise waters and gleaming white sandy beaches would attract anyone I would think.

While Puerto Plata would have been a suitable place to stage it was on the North coast and that would put us even farther from Port-Au-Prince, so that option was quickly eliminated. Barahona, more accurately Santa Cruz de Barahona, was chosen as the best spot to stage ourselves.

Barahona had a continually active port and lots of ecotourism that would provide good cover. It is big in the sugar industry as well, so the port was also a busy commercial one. This would be the real advantage of using a yacht charter in this way. They were all over the place down here and, although not as busy as the Dominican, Haiti was getting more popular.

The massive economic disparity between locals and these "yachties" created a stark chasm of despair that would help motivate our potential attackers.

Once we docked at Port-Au-Prince we would quickly become a ransom target. The good thing is the various groups within the gang operated as private entities to help protect themselves. We knew there was little, if any, communication between these groups. If one group got caught the others would still be free to do their business. That would allow us to lure one group to certain death and hot have to worry about others knowing it was us.

The yacht that had been chartered for us picked us up in Vieques and we set sail to Barahona. Actually, there were no sails involved. This was a high-powered yacht designed for the ecotourism industry. It was still a super yacht, but a little more stripped down due to its focus on ecotours.

The ship itself was about 110 feet long and very capable in the open ocean. It could outrun all but the fastest pursuit boats in the area. Three large motors sort of ran counter to the whole "eco" vibe but that didn't matter to us, or those spending a hundred thousand or so to charter her. This craft would be ideal cover and just the thing to lure the criminals out.

They typically would not come right into the marina to kidnap anyone. They would watch and wait until the people they wanted went out on a tour or even headed to a bar. There is an active and vibrant nightlife scene in Port-Au-Prince. I guess a port city is a port city, no matter the destitution and poverty that surrounds it.

The next day we were moored in a large marina at PAP (Port-Au-Prince) and having a leisurely lunch as we did our best to look like idle rich folk.

We had already been connected to a concierge type service that gave us many options to get out there. We knew there had been prior activity by these gangs around a club called La Reserve. It is a jazzy joint hidden in the forested hills of Petion Ville. We rolled in there after dark and all agreed that if we weren't operating, we would certainly visit this place.

An uneven, rocky path wound its way through the trees with a low voltage string of lights to help guide the way. The path soon opened up into an area filled with small tables and chairs as well as a stand-up bar. The food was top shelf, and we ate well.

We figured there was likely a lookout who worked there that would notify the gang when there was a target or two handy.

We made an acceptable amount of noise as we did our best rendition of friends partying. When it was time to pay up, we made a big deal about coming back the next night and how much fun this was. Hopefully, word would get back to a gang member and they might make their move the next evening.

We spent the next day doing a little training and then prepared ourselves. We knew this would have to be quiet so no guns. That didn't mean no weapons. Each of us had two knives on our person and I had three garottes. We had no idea how many kidnappers there would be, nor did we know if they would try to take one, two or all three of us. We were always ready for anything so none of us was worried.

Chapter 40 Two - Kidnapped

The evening arrived and we were all more than ready. We knew that no matter who or what they had, these amateurs would be no match for three highly trained SEALs. Now it was a matter of ordering waters and non-alcoholic drinks and doing our best to look like any other drunken Americans partying.

As with the previous evening, we were leaving some large tips and making it quite known we were doing it. We felt like we were being watched and decided it would be time to leave soon, and hopefully the attempt would be made. We had another couple of drinks each and then staggered our way down the path. As we got into our vehicle, we noticed two guns pointed at us. One from the back seat and one from the bushes.

We did our best to act scared, but it took real acting. Two amateurs, even with guns, were not going to know what hit them. There was one in the passenger seat with his gun pointed at me and one in the back pointing his weapon at Sonny and Travis. They were so close to us this would be child's play.

We had a code word to use when it was time to pounce and as I hit the brakes hard both "kidnappers" were quickly disarmed. We pulled into a dark spot off the road and did a little convincing.

They told us there was another vehicle with two more men waiting for them about two miles ahead. We believed the story but questioned the number of men.

We beat them up pretty badly and then Sonny and Travis moved out to ambush the others. We were able to communicate with each other using our earwigs so would be in constant communication. Once they headed out, I took the crooks one at a time and used a garrotte to kill them.

I first tied them each to a tree with a gag in their mouth and then sliced though their throats leaving a bloody mess behind. It really was a gruesome sight when I left them. When they were found word would spread quickly.

Sonny and Travis advised they were at the truck, and I could drive up and get them. I drove up the bumpy road in complete darkness and hit the lights when I got close. I will admit to being a little shocked with the scene with which I was greeted. I had made a mess of my two guys, but the boys had taken it to another level. Each man (there were actually four) had been tied to the hood of the vehicle. All four looked like they had been in a war.

Think of the worst, most brutal MMA beating you have seen and multiply that by ten times. The four men were unrecognizable. We cleaned ourselves up, packed up any and all evidence and drove back close to the marina. Two hours later we were kicked back on the boat enjoying an ice-cold beer. Now, we would wait to see what showed up in the news and what we could hear on the streets.

Surprisingly, it took three days for anything to surface.

It wasn't even a large article but there was a photo of my two guys showing their almost decapitated bodies covered in now dried blood. The other four didn't make the paper likely because they were simply TOO messy.

Now it was more wait and see time.

Chapter 40 Three – Backlash?

We spent the next day moored just off the coast. We swam and splashed around in the cerulean blue waters of the Caribbean for most of the day. We knew, due to the lack of intergang communication, the killings would not be traced back to us. We simply had to continue looking rich and unaffected by the conditions surrounding us.

We also needed to select a new nightclub in which to display our wealth. We were told the jet set club bar and restaurant would be a great place to do so. They have multiple VIP sections where one can display their wealth by ordering bottle service at your table.

The concept of paying over 500 dollars for a 75-dollar bottle of booze simply to have it domiciled at your table was ludicrous to us. Sure, it came with your own waitress who held the key to the cage holding the bottle, but it was simply crazy. We knew that to be targets we would need to go there at least twice, if not three times so we readied ourselves for a few long nights.

It was afternoon naps, after training, for all of us to ensure we were well rested and able to remain on high alert for extended periods. The three of us agreed we had to attempt to locate their base of operations so this would be a significantly different, and more dangerous, operation.

We all believed the level of danger would be mitigated by our brash display of wealth which would make the kidnappers keen to get a large ransom rather than actually kill anyone.

It was completely counterintuitive for us to allow ourselves to be captured but that was exactly our plan. We knew the kidnappers would be armed but we had disarmed much more highly trained attackers than these. This was the only way we saw possible for us to gather more information and perhaps even deal a crippling blow to their little cottage "industry."

We looked at a number of clubs where we could attract the most attention and settled on Fubar in Petion-Ville. We decided that prior to heading to this popular nightclub we would enjoy a fresh seafood dinner at Le Coin des Artistes. We prepared for our big night out and got a ride to Le Coin.

On the outside it appeared very Haitian but as we were led to our table it looked more like the courtyard at Pat O'Brien's in New Orleans, also an excellent restaurant and nightspot. We sat at our table and began to peruse the menu. The seafood is transported directly from the fishermen to the restaurant, so it is beyond fresh. The aromas of freshly grilled fish permeate the whole establishment. This might be a rather good gig after all I thought to myself.

As they took our drink orders, we all stuck to virgin cocktails just to be safe, they delivered some fresh crab cakes. We all enjoyed our meals tremendously and were well fed by the time we left for the nightclub.

It was Thursday night, which we would soon find out is jazz night at Fubar. Although this was our first high visibility outing at this club, we still needed to keep our wits about us. We stuck to slowly drinking bottled beer, which came to the table unopened, so there was less chance of anything being spiked. The three of us alternately fended off advances. To be honest, I was a little bit pissed that Sonny and Travis seemed to get more action than I did, a fact that was not lost on them. I had to endure subtle and quiet ribbing for most of the evening on that very subject.

We stuck it out as long as we could until finally getting a ride back to the marina. Taxis is Haiti are also referred to as "tap-taps" and some even operate as buses able to handle 20-30 people at a time. We stuck to the smaller, single group versions as we felt that would increase our chances of being "kidnapped".

We were returned to the marina without incident but were still on high alert as we walked down the dock to our boat. Once we got ourselves back onto the yacht, we sat on the aft sundeck to relax. Now that we were safe and sound on our boat, we enjoyed some Barbancourt Rhum.

Barbancourt is a very tasty rum made from pure sugar cane juice and bottled in Haiti. It is well known as one of the finest rums in the world and has held that distinction for most of its 159-year life. It's quite story, having been established in 1862 by Dupre Barbancourt when he moved from the Cognac region of France to Haiti. Barbancourt rum is Haiti's answer to Scotland's many whisky distilleries.

As we sipped our rums, we discussed how we thought it odd that we heard nothing about the grisly deaths of the first group to attempt to kidnap us.

We hoped that word had been passed amongst the various gang factions but had no way to be certain. We planned our next evening out and then all hit the rack for some well-earned sleep. The gentle rocking of the yacht seemed to really help as I slept like a baby, soundly and for a long time.

I awoke to the sun streaming into my stateroom and decided to jump up and go for a three- or four-mile swim. Nothing particularly challenging, just like a runner might head out for a relaxing morning run. I hopped in off the swim platform, set my target on a lighthouse and began to leisurely slice my way through the gently rolling waters.

I was wary of what was around me as we knew that Haiti was home to the Oceanic Whitetip Sharks, one of the more dangerous to humans.

While most in this area would be juveniles, and not as dangerous, there would also be some mature adults. The Captain had advised that while there had been none spotted in this particular section of water it was still advisable to be aware.

I had knives strapped to each thigh and also a bang stick, just to be safe. The Oceanic Whitetip has attacked more humans than all other shark species combined, so this certainly wasn't the safest water to be in. The good thing was that these sharks spent the bulk of their time in the upper layer of the ocean so being attacked from below, which is typical for most shark species, was not as much of a concern.

Their overly large, white tipped tail could often be spotted out of the water so that was another visual clue that you were being approached. Luckily, they are not pack swimmers, but they still might congregate where there was a food source. They are slow movers as well, a benefit of being the top of the food chain, which could help with defense. Much to my chagrin I did run into a couple, quickly deciding this would be my last distance swim, but they were smaller juveniles so did not bother with me.

It wasn't too long before I was back on the yacht and thankful to be there. The boys gave me a lot of grief about my foray, and I promised that was it for me. I would stick to splashing around in shallower waters where the Whitetips were unlikely to be found.

We got together and did a little self defence training and then all retired for some sleep before our evening out. We had already decided to skip the restaurant and just show up at the club later on.

Chapter 40 Four – Back to Fubar

Finally, it was time to head out and hopefully get kidnapped. We hopped in our new favorite tap-tap and were soon back at Fubar and ready to pretend to party. It was close to 11:00 PM when we rolled up to the door and were pleased to see the place was packed. We really hoped this would be our night as we had big plans for our captors.

We did order bottle service and kept the drinks flowing. We were sure to expend most of the liquor on the various hangers-on and potential suitors while we slowly sipped our own, weaker drinks. As the night wore on, we confirmed with each other that there did appear to be eyes on us this evening.

We began to act increasingly inebriated as the night progressed, dancing with wild abandon and falling all over the place. Finally, we called our ride and hopped into the van. We bounced around as we drove along a rougher than expected road and knew what was next. We asked why we were going this way and, just then from the far rear, we heard the sound of two guns being cocked as the driver said not to try anything stupid.

Well, it was easy to get kidnapped after all. We pulled over and while the two kept their guns trained on us, we were taken out of the vehicle, one at a time.

They used zip ties to bind our wrists and then put us back into the van. They weren't all that experienced as they did not notice that we had each left enough slack in the ties by flexing our wrists to enable escape whenever we wished. They were so unskilled at this that they never even frisked us, assuming we were just your average tourists. A SEAL can do a lot of damage with a ka-bar knife and we each had at least one strapped to a leg.

We rumbled along the rough road for another 7 or 8 minutes and then turned into a driveway that was mostly obscured by large trees. We were then moved inside where we were taken into a dank and dark basement with a dirt floor. It reeked of mould and mildew. We heard the door lock behind us and knew it was only a matter of time before they came back to ask us questions. The most important would be who should they contact to pay the ransom and purchase our release.

About an hour later two of them returned and we heard them fumbling with the locked door. They were surprisingly calm and relaxed as they descended the stairs. Neither appeared to have a weapon so we assumed there must be at least two more fully armed upstairs, perhaps more. We would need to find that out before we could plan our exit. We provided them with a phone number and contact name to a burner cell phone that SECNAV's aide carried with him at all times. Once we passed that along they left us, only returning to provide us with some food and water.

Keeping hostages alive and in decent shape was imperative to their success and they were clearly aware of that fact. The sandwiches were quite tasty and there was plenty of water for all of us. Thankfully, there was no washroom down there nor any place to relieve ourselves.

They advised that if any of us needed to use the washroom we could knock on the door, and we would be allowed up. Dummies! We would be permitted to exit only one at a time and were told if anyone tried anything all three of us would be shot. They would have no clue what was coming so we weren't at all worried about their threat.

Over the course of the next few hours each of us made trips to use the facilities, noting the descriptions of each of the men we could see. Once we had all made our trips, we compared notes and were able to confirm that there were six men up there and perhaps one or two more outside. Honestly, the actual numbers didn't concern us as we were leaving nobody alive and there was no need to gather any additional information.

We had prearranged with SECNAV to tell these guys it would take two days for them to get the cash, but they could definitely get it. That would give us time to take them all out and get ourselves back to a safe place.

Fortunately, there were no drugs in the food or water, so we were all fully functioning, two-legged, weapons of mass destruction. We worked through a few different plans over the next six hours and decided we would move on them in the morning, when our food was brought to us.

I can't speak for Sonny and Travis, but I slept quite well and was up and ready to go bright and early. We positioned Sonny close to the stairs as Travis and I waited across the room. There was a wall on one side of the stairs that blocked the view of anyone on them so that helped our plan a great deal. We heard the lock opening and then watched as the two men descended into the basement. By the time they noticed that they could not see all three of us it was too late.

Sonny tripped one as he stepped off the last step and caught him with a kick to the face as he fell. Before the other could make any sound, he grabbed him by the throat and pulled him down the last two stairs, plunging his knife straight through the man's throat. He left him gurgling to his own death on the now bloodied dirt floor.

Time was at a premium, so we moved quickly but quietly up the stairs. As the first of us reached the top step one of the men upstairs yelled down something to the two guys we had just eliminated. We knew things were about to get hectic and they did. Soon there were fists and knives flying everywhere as we disabled the men as quickly as we could.

Suddenly I heard a loud bang and then felt a searing pain rip through my upper arm. I realized I had been shot and as I turned, I watched Travis almost decapitate the shooter with his knife. We grabbed whatever guns we could see and prepared to check outside as Sonny applied a tourniquet, fashioned from his shirt to my arm. It hurt, but the pain was bearable. I sensed the slug had missed any bones and was likely a through and through. Hopefully, that was indeed the case as going to a hospital with a gunshot wound would not be a clever idea in this place.

Once the whole crew was disabled, we added a few grisly touches and then tied two of them to the back of their own vehicle. We drove back closer to the road where the vehicle could be found quickly but left us enough escape time to get back to the yacht. There was enough gasoline and oil at the shack that we were able to fashion a delayed blast to obliterate their lair.

We had left the vehicle and were moving through the trees and brush quickly as the cabin was blown sky high. We had no idea if the local police were involved with these guys or what the deal was so we stayed as out of sight as we could.

Finally, we were close to the marina, and I waited as Sonny and Travis returned to the yacht and then brought the small tender back to move me. My arm and shoulder were starting to hurt more now that the adrenaline was no longer coursing through my veins, but it was still tolerable. As soon as we got to the yacht Sonny took me down to my stateroom while Travis grabbed the first aid kit.

Being a superyacht, they had an extensive kit on board, so I wasn't at all worried. Besides, I had seen Travis perform an emergency tracheotomy in the field using duct tape and a bic pen that saved a man's life. He had also set and splinted numerous broken bones in his day as well as cauterized and bandaged a number of GSW's. As far as I was concerned. He was practically a doctor anyway.

Travis took a quick look and confirmed that it was indeed a through and through so there was no slug to worry about. That was good news as, even for a SEAL, having someone digging around inside a hole in your arm was a painful experience without anesthesia. Nevertheless, disinfecting the area and the wound wasn't exactly a walk in the park either. I gritted my teeth as he did his best to be quick, but thorough.

Ten minutes later I took a couple of Tylenol 3's and sacked out. The throbbing in my arm to the rhythm of my heart was annoying but tolerable.

I had been through worse I recalled as I drifted off to sleep.

Chapter 40 Five – Business As Usual?

I awoke a little later than normal in the morning when I rolled onto the side on which I had been shot. The sudden pain woke me immediately and the whole thing came flooding back. I began to think what I could have done differently to avoid being shot. I came up with little and left it at the fact that ours were dangerous jobs and getting shot was a workplace hazard that was not ever completely avoidable.

We knew the message had been sent and we discussed that fact around the table as we ate some breakfast. We decided to lay low and just hang on the yacht for a couple of days and see what happened. We would head into PAP tomorrow and the day after and see what was in the news. I spent that entire day watching those two clowns splash around in the water as I remained on the deck and kept up a shark watch. The ocean is loaded with bacteria so swimming with a semi-open wound would not be a brilliant plan.

We finished up our dinner and then just lounged around on the sun deck. I marvelled at the sunset as it slowly began to reveal itself. It looked like one of those travel posters or movie ads. I watched, mesmerized, as the glowing red ball of light drifted lazily downward, edging closer and closer to the horizon. The sun filtered through a broken, cloudy sky that made the event that much more impressive.

It completely held my gaze as it moved lower and lower and was seemingly extinguished when it hit the water and disappeared. It was certainly a different sunset than when watching from Huntington Beach.

We decided to visit the Iron Market the next day. It's a covered bazaar that began around 1891. The market itself is an impressive sight to see. It was originally built as a train station with two massive iron halls. Most refer to it as stunning Victorian architecture with a Caribbean flavour. The large majority of the stalls, built with row upon row of rickety wooden tables, are kept by women. At almost 20,000 square feet it is a massive market with a cacophony of sound that absolutely assaults your senses.

There are many street food vendors, and it seems like every tenth stall has a juicing machine going nonstop. If one were hungry, and wanting to sample, you could fill up on everything from Caribbean pasties to fried plantains in minutes. Personal recipe stews of varying types are also immensely popular in the market, and elsewhere.

The market itself had taken a real beating in recent years. The 2010 Haiti earthquake inflicted a great deal of damage and that was preceded by a massive fire in 2008. As recently as 2018 it was hit with another fire that destroyed one of the two large halls. Haiti is nothing if not resilient and things are moving back to normal.

While the rural housing is virtually all two room "homes" made with mud walls and floors and thatched roofs, housing in Port Au Prince itself presents every color of the rainbow. What it lacks in architectural detail it makes up for in color. The hillside, from a distance, appears to be one massive painted canvas.

As you move closer and closer, the details begin to reveal themselves. The houses are almost stacked on top of one another. Each one a wilder and more unique color than the one next door.

There is a downside, however. At one million people, this capital city of Haiti is one of the largest cities in the world living without benefit of a central sewage system. Most houses have no running water and if there is water flowing through the pipes it is deemed unfit for human consumption.

The whole metro area of PAP now houses something on the order of 3 million people. Most of them use outhouses with that waste draining into canals, ditches, and other dumping ground. The building of any type of sewage treatment system is solely at the mercy of the people and countries who donate to Haiti. While the problem will not be solved tomorrow, they do appear to be making headway. The whole situation was a stark reminder of how anxious I now was to return home. The guys were of the same mind.

It wasn't until the fourth day after our kidnapping that a few snippets of information appeared in the news. There was some chatter at neighboring tables we were able to make out and a little news in a small local paper, but that was about it. We all began to wonder if this ransom business was just that, a local business?

The following day when we were lounging on the yacht was when the satellite phone rang. We were to return to our base at the San Juan water and Beach Club Hotel in Puerto Rico. There was something up for sure.

There was no further discussion and no other directions given. The next day we were all back in our rooms at the hotel and awaiting instruction. Perhaps our message was strong enough or it could be something entirely different. We had no choice but to wait to find out.

We were all shocked when the aide we had been dealing with showed up on a tender two days later. He was there to brief us on what was going to happen next. The four of us adjourned to the dining salon, which was isolated on the middle level of the yacht.

He began by pointing out to us that the US had been the largest donor of relief funds to Haiti since 1973. In the eight years preceding 2003 the US had sent roughly $850 million in aid to Haiti.

Since 2004, another $ 600 million has been provided. The main goals of that cash were to improve security, governance, enforce the rule of law, and meet basic human needs.

Apparently, our country was not impressed with the lack of results and the growing kidnapping "business" was one of those concerns. US intelligence had determined that the police were corrupt and, not only financially benefitting from a tax on kidnappers, but even perpetrating some acts themselves.

Since mid 2021, when the Haitian President Moise was assassinated, there has been a great deal of concern. Moise was an entrepreneur and politician who had been elected in 2017. You had to be committed to public service to take that position as the remuneration is a mere $3,782 USD per annum.

Since the US announced that charges are being laid against a second man involved in Moise's killing they have stepped up intelligence in the area. They have made contact with Ariel Henry, who is the acting leader of Haiti. He is a neurosurgeon as well as a politician.

Henry was recently banned from leaving the country as there is an investigation underway regarding his possible involvement in Moise's death. He apparently had multiple phone calls with Joseph Badio, who is a key suspect in the murder.

Henry himself has already survived an attempted assassination that occurred at a ceremony celebrating the country's independence. The US is still unclear if his pledge to crack down on the powerful gangs blamed for many of the kidnappings and other crimes is real or just smoke and mirrors. Was it the gangs trying get rid of him, possibly a political rival or maybe even the police? In Haiti, it was difficult to determine who your enemies were.

What state does know is that Haiti absolutely depends on the continued monetary support from the US. They are going to use that need to force Henry's cooperation, at least while he is in power. There is no election scheduled and it remains unclear as to when or if one will be held. The President has decided that action needs to be taken sooner rather than later.

Sonny, Travis, and I will be joined by six more operators. We will be infiltrating the police force along with a hundred others.

The other hundred are part of the US contribution to baling out Haiti while we will be the only ones digging into the corruption angle.

The Haitian National Police Force is the only group that can apply and enforce the law since the Haitian army was disbanded in 1995.

One of their main challenges is that they are most often outgunned and, outgassed, by gangs like the 400 Mawozo and others. The gangs control the movement of fuels around the country and even the police have a tough time. The gangs have more powerful vehicles, faster motorcycles, and better guns. The challenge was an immense one and the nine of us were going to be the bleeding edge of the sword.

The force consists of a little more than 12,000 officers, most of whom can still be classed as rookies. Countries including the US and Canada have provided resources and training but in such a poor country, corruption is difficult to block. This was deemed the bast way possible.

We would all gather intelligence, while preventing as much crime within the ranks as possible, and report regularly. It didn't seem like a mission for a bunch of door-kickers like us but there certainly are extenuating circumstances. In these situations, there is typically a group of powerful people who drive the balance of the evildoers. We expected that would be exactly the same case here.

The interesting part is that, based on all intelligence gathered to date, there are two heads of the snake. One male and one female. The female Marie-Jean Joseph seemed to be the more dangerous of the two.

She had been in the military and quickly risen through the ranks. She was known as ruthless and as close to a sociopath as one could be and still live a relatively normal life.

The top male in the force is Francois Georges. He is also a force with which to be reckoned but deemed nowhere near as unpredictable as Marie-Jean. The French influence permeates Haitian culture, even though France wanted no such association. When the French government finally ended slavery, the freed slaves needed to be given last names. France tried to prevent them using French names as surnames but were unsuccessful. Today many Haitian names relate directly to the French language.

We worked hard with our team devising a plan before entering the academy for a brief training time that police from other countries or military converts had to attend. It was more about culture and language than anything else but there was also a small gang component. For the first time before starting a mission I was concerned about the outcome. After all, this wasn't kicking in doors and shooting up the bad guys. We would have to work with them to infiltrate fully. It would not be easy.

Chapter 40 Six – Training

Within a few weeks we were all installed in the training facility. We had learned this section was led by Canada and included things like uncovering top skills in recruits so they could be placed where they might have the greatest success. There was a "train-the-trainer" program for senior officers and others who would be charged with growing the force. Once we were settled in, the training in most aspects was being handled by Canadians or Americans.

The UN has stated multiple times that training of Haiti's national police force is paramount to stabilizing the geopolitical situation in the region. Canada had committed to building a training academy in Haiti almost six years ago but the politics in that country are such a mess that after twelve years nothing has been built.

Haitian police are still training in temporary facilities connected to the original academy. That would likely help us make the connections we needed and keep our own lines of communication open. We had already decided that our end goal would be for me to make myself known so that I might ingratiate myself to Marie-Jean while Travis worked his own way towards Francois Georges.

It was similar to working my way up the cartel ranks but I would have to be much more strategic here. Running around killing people certainly would not help. Knowing that Marie-Jean had been in the military and had been quite a fighter herself we knew that I should go almost full out at the academy. She would hopefully become interested in me as we worked through our training. I would make certain of that.

Training was fairly basic for the first week. It wasn't like we were un-trained recruits, so we got into some relatively series things right out of the gate. I always liked the afternoon sessions as that was when all the physical training got going. There was weapons training as well as takedown techniques and other hand-to-hand tactics at which I excelled.

The first day of hand-to-hand tactics was almost humorous for me. I knew I couldn't make the instructor look too bad, but I had a tough time not fighting at 100%. Sometimes, my subconscious took over and I had to restrain myself before taking it too far. Everyone was padded up pretty well, so I just had to make sure I didn't torque a limb too much and break it.

It was a relief to head over to the gun range. There was no reason for me not to do my best there, so that's exactly what I did. I shot the lights out with both hands during pistol work at 25 and 50 yards. My groupings were the best of any of the targets at the end of the session.

We then moved onto rifles, where it only took one round for me to be designated as a sniper. I would never describe the first rifle we trained with as a true sniper rifle.

The Barrett M82 was designed more as an anti-material rifle. With its 10-round magazine of .50 calibre ammunition you could easily destroy sensitive equipment, vehicles, even parked aircraft. It was used against personnel as well as it could shoot exceptionally long range and penetrate things like bricks and concrete. Even though the muzzle was said to absorb 70% of the recoil, it still provided a decent kick when fired.

The true sniper rifle was next and that was a Sako TRG 42. This is the company that made my favorite hunting rifle I used at home, the Tikka T3. They are an extremely reliable and accurate bolt action rifle that can be chambered in either a .300 Winchester Magnum or a .338 Lapua Magnum. I preferred the latter. As I was quite familiar with the weapon, I fully embraced the practice of firing it.

The instructors seemed extremely impressed at my center ring accuracy at 200, 500 and 1,000 yards. The nameplate range of the weapon, chambered with the .338 Lapua, is 1,500 metres which is a little over 1,600 yards. It was a formidable tool and one I really respected. Sure, there are many others that work almost as well, including the old standby .22-250 magnums that were often used by SWAT, but this was a favorite of mine.

Our training lasted only four weeks and in that time half of us had been selected for tactical team duty. The others purposely dialed it down a notch so they would be placed in regular units. I knew I was already being noticed so it was a matter of playing my cards well from here on to get closer and closer to M J Joseph. I had no idea how much time it would take but needed to do everything I could to speed things up.

Chapter 40 Seven – Making Inroads

Now that we were all working in our units, we had to meet covertly to ensure we were not discovered. It was in week three when I first was exposed to something not quite kosher in my tactical unit. I was anxious to meet with the guys and see if they were getting any strange vibes where they were working. I felt quite safe having both Sonny and Travis working on tactical unit one with me, but we still had to be careful. There were two more on the second tac unit as well.

We had been assigned to run a surveillance operation on two high-ranking government officials. The word was that they were corrupt, and we were to gather as much intel as possible. We all thought it odd that a tac team was being used like the CIA, but it was Haiti after all, the place was just downright strange in a lot of ways. There were two intelligence officers with us who I assumed reported straight to the top based on their deportment and behaviour.

We knew there was corruption in the ranks but spying on government folks like this was just too Watergate for me. We each maintained accurate notes and reported daily to our team lead. At the same time, we were also sharing information with each other and our own government. We would have to catch them in the act of doing something illegal and gather proof along with having backup witnesses.

Because of that fact the three of us were never too far from each other. Conveniently, tac team one only had eight members so doing that was not terribly difficult.

I hoped that I would not have to step too far over the line to get on Marie-Jean's radar and begin my climb to the top. I suppose that was the drawback to being recognized as a great sniper. If something were going to happen, I might be called upon. THAT would make for an exceedingly tricky situation.

We followed the two people we were tasked with keeping an eye on to FUBAR. A club we were familiar with, so at least we already knew where everything was and how best to keep an eye on things. It was still early so it was more of a dinner crowd than the nightclub bunch. I received orders to stake out some higher ground where I could keep an eye on the back entrance. The voice in my earpiece directed me to get my rifle setup in case there were any issues. I really, really hoped that nothing developed.

I was a good enough shot that I could definitely injure without killing and then blame it on movement or something similar. I sat silently in my perch, concealed by the shrubbery around me, but still maintaining a clear line of sight to the exit.

We had been in place for almost two hours when I was told there was a man leaving by the back door in a dark coat, wearing a beige fedora, and he was my target. Luckily, I was told to wound him only so that was a relief.

As he stepped out of the door, I hit him in the upper arm with one shot. He went down but I knew there was no way he was dying or anything. I had taken extra care to miss his shoulder due to the damage that would cause. After I made the shot, I quickly broke down my rifle into its pack and returned to our vehicle.

As I got there, two of the guys had the dude I had shot and another fellow with them. Both were hooded and their hands were zip tied behind their backs. They were pushed into the rear of the van, we all got in, and we drove off in no particular hurry. The driver took his time and after about 20 minutes we rolled into a driveway. Someone outside opened the back doors, took the two men out and then slammed the doors shut. No words were exchanged, as we returned to our station, but there were quite a few sideways glances.

It wasn't until the next day when we were told the two men were part of the 400 Mawozo's and they had been looking to broker a truce with a rival gang. It seemed something was a bit off in the explanation, but we let it go for now. We felt we would be read into the overall plan at some point.

Chapter 40 Eight – We Are On The Team

It was three days later when our team lead took me, Sonny, and Travis aside and said we needed to have a chat. We were in a room alone and he scanned us and asked if we really knew what was happening in Haiti. Travis took the lead and said it looked like there was real money to be made here, perhaps over and above our regular pay. That was what got us moving upwards and moving toward trusted criminal status.

He said that we had just participated in an illegal kidnapping, and it had all been caught on tape. We would be wise to keep the information to ourselves and perhaps we would become full participants in their little venture. They would decide when the time was right and, until then, we were to keep our noses clean and follow orders.

That was exactly what we did. As a result, we had extraordinarily little to report whenever we were discussing things. Some of the other guys had inklings that there were things going on. There were times when they were singled out and either left behind or sent on wild goose chases while others in their units were up to something different.

We were quite happy when the whole unit decided a night out was in order. We had the upcoming Sunday and Monday off, so we had arranged to meet at the club to eat and then party on Sunday night.

It was agreed that we would all meet at Barak, which is a sports bar that apparently also has outstanding food. Their TVs were set up to watch multiple sports and they usually had some sort of MMA or boxing in one section.

We all met around the corner from the station and took a couple of vans to the club. Everyone was dressed casually, and it was the first time I had seen the rest of the group in street clothes. Some didn't look too comfortable out of uniform and without the usual vests, weapons, and belts. We walked in mostly together and were shown to a large table in a section in the rear. It was half inside and half outside. You could already see stars in the sky and there was a broken view of the harbor.

I scanned the club and noticed what looked to be quite a few U.N. forces folks hanging around at the pool tables. I supposed that made sense as even crooked law enforcement people like to congregate with other law enforcement folks. Safety in numbers and that sort of thing. We had a great dinner, and the food was exceptionally good. Once we were all done, we gravitated in two groups to other parts of the club.

Sony and Travis wanted to play some pool so one of them put a couple of coins on the corner of a table to signify they had next game.

I wasn't much for the game myself but stood there and watched while I dreamed of being on a surfboard somewhere. As I walked towards the ladies' room, I was shocked to feel a hand slap my ass. I spun around quickly, and when I realized it was nobody I knew, I grabbed his hand and twisted quickly to immobilize him.

As I held him that way our faces were close and I looked him in the eye and said, "I'm sure that was an accident and you're very sorry, no?" He smiled at me and somehow got his other hand around, to once more hit my ass, and said, "no."

That was enough for me. I took him down to the ground in one quick move and when he tried to break the hold, I knew he had training. Didn't matter much as I used his feeble attempt to gain extra leverage and now, I was standing above him. His hand was immobilized in my grip and my boot was on his throat. I smiled down at him and said if he makes one more move, I'll snap his wrist and then beat him within an inch of his life. I pressed my foot down a little harder and he stopped trying to speak.

I let him up and was a little surprised when he said, "Okay, okay. I'm sorry, I won't do it again." I glared at him and suggested he might not want to do that to any other woman either. As I continued walking, my back to him, I heard him mumble something about crooked cops.

I let it go and just kept walking. Thankfully, there were no other shenanigans that night and we all got back to where we were staying safely and without further incident.

At our morning meeting the next day we heard about our antics at the club. The team lead seemed pissed that anything had happened at all. I tried to explain but he cut me off and said that we were to stay out of trouble, ALL of us. A few other guys glared at me like I had done something wrong. I wasn't impressed.

It took another couple of weeks of the typical grunt work until our unit was tasked to carry out a mission. There was a drug cartel that was trying to move in on the 400 Mawozo territory and the local police did not want a gang war raging in their streets. We were given photos and an information package on the rivals and told to capture them, kill them, whatever worked.

We knew this was our first test of whether we were corruptible or not.

It's not like we were about to kill anybody innocent or anything, but it did seem odd that police were being used to eliminate one gang but leave the other untouched.

When the three of us debriefed we easily agreed that it looked like the police were protecting the Mawozo.

Chapter 40 Nine – Bang, Bang

We were told that we were to dress as civilians and keep our weapons as hidden as possible. In seven hours, the gang was going to be moving in on the Mawozo territory and we would take them out when they got close. We knew they would be heavily armed and if we did not play our cards right there would a firefight. We were told to accomplish this as quietly as possible.

When the time was near, we took up a position around a tight corner on the only road they could use. One side of the road was a steep drop off to the ocean and the other was a high rocky cliff. Once they came around the corner, they would be trapped. We were told that "arranging" an accident was no good, we needed to kill them all and leave the bodies and vehicles to be found in the morning. Obviously, they wanted a message sent to others who might have similar ideas. It sure would have been much simpler to just blow them off the road and watch as they crashed to their death.

We knew, if properly carried out, this might be a way for us to get one or two steps closer to Marie-Jean and her partner in crime, Francois Georges. As the leaders of the Haitian National Police Force, they would be able to do just about anything short of a coup without raising too many eyebrows.

It was clear, based on this action, that the Mawozo either had something on the two leaders or they were already in bed with them.

Our weapons all were fitted with sound suppressors so the pop-pop-pop of the rifle shots would barely be heard. We were prepared to be able to take them all out without any of them getting a shot off.

We positioned our vehicle, as if broken down, to block the roadway. I was chosen as the one to be the driver in distress. I wasn't past the point of being pissed off that the only woman had to be the one who couldn't get her car working. I would razz the boys about it later on and maybe challenge one of them to fix a car or two. My father had taught be all about vehicles and, when I was younger, we had even rebuilt a hot rod together. I was quite certain I knew more about cars than any of these clowns.

I had the hood of the car open and was wearing a loose jacket, which effectively concealed my two pistols. I would approach the drivers' side of their vehicle once they stopped, and as the boys hit the rear doors, I would pop whoever was in the front seats at the same time.

We had left a lookout about five miles back down the road who had already confirmed there was only the one vehicle. For some reason, they expected no trouble which I found quite odd.

I suppose the gangs down here figured they operated with impunity. You just never knew who was affiliated with whom, however.

I readied myself as I heard a vehicle approaching. I watched from next to my open hood as they scanned the area. I was surprised that the passenger at least did not exit the vehicle as I walked towards them. The windows were down as I got close to the door, and I saw Travis at the rear. As I began to explain that my car had broken down, I pulled out a pistol in each hand and shot them both in the head simultaneously. Each bullet fulfilled its lethal purpose and they both slumped forward in their seats. There was no need to check for life as I was using mushroom slugs and the projectiles entered right in the middle of each forehead. I knew there was a baseball sized hole in the back of their skulls.

At virtually the same time, I heard a number of pops from the rear of the vehicle. The whole event was over in mere seconds. We left the driver and passenger slumped in their seats where I had shot them. The boys dragged the others out into the roadway, put a few more bullets in each and we were on our way.

We returned to our vehicle and headed back to our makeshift station like business as usual.

When we stepped through the doors, I was a little shocked to see Marie-Jean already in the room. I was wondering if the three of us were about to be staring down the barrels of a few guns.

I need not have worried. MJ announced that we had just performed a great service for the country and that we had earned a couple of days of R & R. We were all told to pack some casual clothes and meet back here in three hours. We were headed over to Marie-Jean's "compound" for a little party. I was pleased when, as we were all leaving, Marie-Jean called me aside.

She looked me in the eye and said that I had done a wonderful job and she heard that I am an exceptional sniper and shooter.

One of the guys had already relayed to her that I had shot both driver and passenger directly in the centre of the forehead, one with each hand. She said how glad she was that I was part of the team and she looked forward to more success from me.

It appeared to be the next step in trust of me and perhaps moved me closer to the inner, corrupt, circle. Although one could never be certain.

Chapter Fifty – Really Part Of The Team

We arrived at the compound, which could more accurately be described as a mansion, and exited the vans. Everyone was pretty laid back and there were tubs of Prestige Lager on ice everywhere. Prestige is actually known as the national beer of Haiti and even won some awards around the world. I was surprised to see it was bottled in those stubby style, old-school bottles. I didn`t even know those were made any longer. I grabbed one, took a sip and noticed it had a slightly salty taste to it, but it was still a good beer, and ice cold.

The beer is brewed right in Port-Au-Prince at the Brasserie Nationale D Haiti. It is now 95% owned by Heineken who recently purchased the corporation. We would later be taken on a tour of the plant, and I was surprised to see it looked like a cross between a prison and a manufacturing plant and not at all like a brewery. Razor wire topped concrete walls gave it the prison look. It appeared they took their liquor quite seriously. I figured certain that the police force was involved in some sort of graft there as well.

It didn't take a great deal of time for the party to really get rocking. These boys knew how to cut loose. Travis, Sonny, and I did our utmost to appear to be consuming similar quantities of alcohol without actually doing so. We had agreed it would be best for us to keep our wits about us. That turned out to be an excellent plan when I was approached later on.

I was directed into the house and back to what looked to be an office.

As I stepped though the doors, I was again greeted my Marie-Jean who was seated next to none other than Francois Georges. She waived me over to a chair cross from them and the guards closed and locked the doors when I sat.

She held my gaze with her own steely look as she slowly said, "I have been watching you," in a thick French accent. I was immediately on edge and quickly scanned the room. She noticed and added, "Don't worry Ma Cherie, it is just us." I expect that you have figured out why we had your team assassinate those drug dealers? I nodded and said, "I assume because they were breaking the law."

Her look became stern as she switched on the television and said, "Do not be so sure of that." I watched as the TV came to life and it was a split screen from two cameras. I watched as she narrated for us. Only a professional killer could do something like this, and I believe that is exactly what you are. We all watched me train both my weapons on the driver and passenger and simultaneously deliver perfect kill shots. "Very impressive," she added.

I have a proposition for you. We want you to join our team. We will make you wealthy beyond your wildest dreams and you will want for nothing. Before you provide your answer, you should know that the video we have, clearly shows you breaking the law and carrying out a public execution. In Haiti, that gets you the death penalty.

In my head I was thinking she has that all backwards. I calmly responded, "Who said I would not want to be on the team?" "I knew what we were doing, it was a little too obvious based on those circumstances." "I would love to participate in what you are doing and am ready to hear any details you wish to provide." Francois grabbed drinks for all three of us and MJ began to explain.

The country of Haiti is a mess. It has been overrun by criminals and the drug dealers have caused a great deal of pain. We decided, once in power, that it would be best to form an alliance with one of these groups. We had arrested a number of people who we knew were higher up in the 400 Mawozo's. We held them in a spot like your Guantanamo Bay facility where you incarcerate people you consider terrorists.

It took some persuading but, after a few weeks of "discussion," we had an agreement in place. We would protect them and their business and in return they would deliver to us 50% of the fruits of their labor.

They sacrifice a few of their own men for us to arrest and charge every now and then so everything looks legitimate and that was that. I was committing as much of the discussion as I could to memory, but we would have to, at some point, get this recorded.

When we were done talking, she waived over our team lead and said that I was fully on board. Of course, I knew that she would have him keeping an even closer eye on me now, but that knowledge would keep me sharp. I knew that I could get out of the country and back to safety if she ever wanted to move on me, but it was still a touchy situation.

Chapter Fifty 1 – Building The File

From that meeting forward, we were gathering absolutely as much information as we could. We each had small cell phones that uploaded photo files and documents directly to the cloud and then removed all traces of them from those phones. They worked almost like a slave unit to a remote server and there was no way to make that connection without the right biometrics plus passcodes.

We were shocked at how much these people were involved in and how broad their sphere of corruption was. In appeared that at least 25% of the National Police Force was corrupt and it was safe to assume there was another 25% of which we were not aware.

They were into drugs, money laundering for other cartels, illegal weapons smuggling, kidnapping, and human trafficking. It was the latter that really got me worked up. The women they were taking and selling, or staffing their brothels with, were not much more than children. We would come to discover that some were as young as fourteen years old. We would also find out that many of the corrupt officers had virtually free access to these brothels. Some were even used to break in the girls.

The protection and manpower the police offered varied as to the nature of the business.

I had no idea how large the Mawozo's were nor that they were involved in so many different things. I knew, for my own sanity, that all bets would be off if I had a chance to save these young women. I figured that if a few more bodies were disposed of while we were gathering intel that would be no big deal. The more information we acquired the deeper it seemed the corrupt officers were involved. It was like Mexico in the old days when the Federales were every bit as crooked as the criminals. We were going to clean this mess up one way or another.

It took a couple of months but the three of us were finally brought in on the trafficking side of things. With Miami so close to the North and Central and South America to the South there was a large tourist trade to access from Haiti. The Dominican Republic and its beaches attracted large numbers of tourists but taking women from so close would bring too much heat on them.

They seemed to have a connection to Venezuela and Columbia as there were many women from that region. They also didn't shy away from gabbing local girls and putting them to work as well. The following week Sonny and Travis were invited to another party. They were told there would be plenty of women that would do anything they wanted. They were able to get me an invite too when they convinced the boss that I was gay.

We arrived at the location given on the night of the party and were a little surprised it was a large hotel. Once we got inside it became crystal clear it was being used as a brothel full time. I supposed when you didn't have to worry about the police you could set up anywhere. It was actually quite a nice-looking hotel inside and out. It would show up as a 3 ½ stars as far as I could tell.

We were directed into a large ballroom that was already packed with people and loud music playing. It was a full-time club based on the décor and layout. The ladies present were a real variety of shapes, sizes, and color, all dressed differently. They were prepared to cater to anyone. As the night progressed, we were able to find out that the girls all lived in the hotel, and this was by far the largest of these venues. There were two to a room and while one was "entertaining" a guest the other would simply party and dance downstairs.

There were bouncers and doormen but not the numbers one would expect. I supposed that with so many policemen partaking of the amenities, they weren't overly concerned. That would certainly be their downfall when the crap hit THIS fan. There were no less than a dozen men I wanted to take out right then and there, but I kept my emotions in check. It was difficult to watch and be a part of in this way.

It was another two weeks before there were substantial military assets in place to execute the plan. There would be a simultaneous grab of Marie-Jean and Francois Georges, at the same time the hotels would be completely sealed and raided. Our goal was to protect the innocents so there would need to be some stealth.

Then suddenly absolutely everything changed!

Chapter Fifty 2 – The World Changed Our Plans

For the second time this year we were pulled from a mission. No warning, no initial reason. The three of us were extracted during a raid with our team that had clearly been setup by someone in the USA.

Sonny, Travis, and I were scooped up and raced out of Haiti post-haste. We were told only that there had been a significant event and that we were needed elsewhere.

24 hours later we were in the same room at Coronado where many of our missions had started. To no one's surprise, SECNAV strode through the door. He turned to lock it and started with an "as usual, this is ALL highly confidential."

We had heard rumblings about Russia and Ukraine but, until this briefing, had no idea what was really happening. The crazy buggers were invading Ukraine. We, much like our government, had assumed that the buildup of troops and all the rocket tests was just sabre-rattling by the self declared President-For-Life.

That was not the case at all. Russian troops were advancing on all major Ukrainian cities.

They were being shelled mercilessly, with the Russians even targeting civilian targets. Tom explained that virtually every other country was closing ranks now and implementing sanctions as well as providing Ukraine with weapons, food, and defenses.

As Ukraine is not a NATO country there were no troops headed that way at the moment. There was also the leader's threat that anyone who intervenes will see "consequences like you could never imagine." That was taken to be his threat to turn to nuclear weapons. Hollow or not, the threat had to be taken seriously.

With the nuclear proliferation that had been going on in so many countries there was enough nuclear armament to destroy the whole planet three or four times over now. Mankind had the power to absolutely destroy the whole planet and it would be one large nuclear wasteland if anything ever started. It would not be at all like those movies where in some post-apocalyptic world there were pockets of human beings left alive, and the planet would get repopulated. Nope, that would never be the case. There will not be one living thing left on this earth if nuclear war begins.

As far as I was concerned, and I hoped I was correct, nukes were like torture. It was the threat alone that did the most damage. Like Hitler and Mussolini before him, Vladimir seemed suddenly bent on expanding his territory.

He wanted to see the USSR reborn and may stop at nothing to achieve that end. He did have his allies including North Korea, Belarus, Syria, and a couple of others, but the absence of support from China gave the US some hope there may be a diplomatic solution.

SECNAV went on to explain that this was a very, very volatile, and dangerous situation and the whole planet was at risk. Hundreds of countries had already imposed sanctions on Russia, assets were being frozen, the assets of wealthy Russian oligarchs were being seized.

Thus far, none of this seems to have affected Vladimir's resolve.

That was where we came in. I already did not like the sounds of this, but I knew that I would do whatever my country required of me. I just had no idea what exactly that would be.

There were many countries concerned about what was happening to Ukraine but none more concerned than Austria, Poland, Romania Turkey and the Baltic states of Latvia and Estonia.

They all had every right to be concerned. They had watched as communism tried to scoop up surrounding democratic states one way or another. Then came the biggest shock of my life.

Tom looked at us and said that traditional tactics were impossible here and the US had to be concerned with the world court.

Adding ANY fuel to this fire could have dire consequences for most of our planet. It had been decided there was only one way to remedy the situation. As difficult a challenge as it would be, Vladimir needed to be taken out. He was cocky enough that he still operated with impunity and was frequently in the public eye. Dictators often think they are untouchable, I saw that with some of the drug lords I took down.

His own disdain for anything non-Russian and his assumption that they were all weak would be his downfall. The Russian people were by no means fully behind what he was doing to Ukraine. They had experienced terrible living conditions after Gorbachev dissolved the USSR in 1991.

Even though the Russian constitution declared them a democratic, federative, law-based state in 1993 the Communist Party still exists and is the second largest party in the country.

Oddly, Russia's current political system is modeled after the country they despise the most, the United States. As in the US, there are three branches of government: legislative, executive, and judicial. If you ask any US politician, they will tell you the Russians blur the lines between those branches.

Of course, they will also tell you that NEVER happens here at home!

Chapter Fifty 3 – The Plan

It did not take long for SECNAV to lay out the plan. It was imperative that Vlad be eliminated, and we were the ones who were going to accomplish it. It became incredibly quiet in that room as the three of us each looked at one another like he was crazy.

Tom brought up a large projected map onto the wall with Russia at the center. He started by saying that Vladimir's own hubris and narcissism would act in our favor. Even though he had basically plunged his country into a war that the majority of the population did not want, he still maintained a rather "regular" routine. He was certainly staying closer to home the majority of the time, but he still crossed the border into Belarus and Kazakhstan from time to time.

Belarus was an obvious ally, but Kazakhstan made sense too. Most recently more than 85% of Kazakhs were said to view Russia in a favorable light. Close to 90% of Kazakh citizens wanted to have a better relationship with Russia. Thanks to a recent high-level defection of a Russian official, the President was aware that there was one particular Kazakh that Vladimir took a special interest in!

Much like the odd US President, Vlad also had an eye for the ladies.

Although divorced, he is known to be seeing Alina Kabaeva. It is even rumored they had twins together. I find it ludicrous to think that the 69-year-old Russian has a gorgeous 38-year-old girlfriend, but he still needs something on the side. Typical of men like him, I supposed.

Kabaeva was more than your average pretty faced, arm candy though. She was a world class gymnast and literally had medals from the Olympics, World Championships and European Championships falling out of drawers. She is also referred to as media manager and a Russian politician.

Tom went on to explain that this side piece of his might be the perfect way to orchestrate his downfall.

We were going to get ourselves into Kazakhstan, get to the location on the list of most likely spots he would meet her and take him out there. It would not be easy and may be a suicide mission, so Tom looked at each one of us to see if we were in. He was clear that if we chose not to accept there would be NO issues with him or anyone else. If we did accept, we would meet back at this room tomorrow with two Russian specialists.

To none of our surprise, or SECNAV's surprise, we all readily agreed. We didn't really discuss it too much after that. We ate our grub, had a workout, and then hit the rack knowing we would all be awake early. And we were.

The weight of what we were being asked to do was not lost any of us. Saying the fate of the free world was now on our shoulders was not a stretch.

We met back in the room and there were two specialists waiting for us. A man and a woman, both of whom looked like they were from Russia's part of the world. They introduced themselves as Piotr and Luba and explained they had all the information we would need. The thing to decide today would be best method and location of access.

Although Kabaeva lived in the Kazakh capital of Nur-Sultan that was a little far from the Russian border. As such, they often met in the city of Oral also known as Uralsk. It is in Northwestern Kazakhstan and much closer to the border with Russia. It has a population of a little over 275,000 with about 2/3 of them Kazakhs and the balance Russian.

We were told that Vladimir had been "visiting" that area for many years, but this new woman was a more recent development. At first it was thought he was meeting Kabaeva there to keep things private but that turned out not to be the case. The woman he was meeting was even younger than Kabaeva. What a pig.

We looked at various points of access and decided to map our way out first. We agreed that Turkey, being a good US ally, would be the best spot from which to get back home. Although perilously close to Syria and Iraq, Turkey was the most favorable spot. In many ways the proximity of Iraq and Syria were two of the big reasons that Turkey remained a US supporter and friend. The logistics of our exfil could be worked out later, right now we needed to decide exactly how we would get there.

We needed to figure out our way in. We would stage ourselves in Turkey where we would be loaded onto a long range, small sized, stealth bomber. Flying at maximum altitude, the plane was unable to be tracked or identified by any existing mechanisms. We would perform a HALO jump (High Altitude Low Opening), perfected by the SEALs, when the plane dipped down below 40,000 feet just long enough for us to jump. The pilot would immediately take it back up and head home.

We completed all our planning and then waited for intelligence to report back while we remained fully prepared. It was difficult to be on the edge like that, ready to go on five minutes notice but that was the life we had chosen.

We just trained, reviewed maps and strategies, and talked about getting in and out. Piotr and Luba had provided a great deal of information as well as three key contacts in Kazakhstan who could help us get out.

Finally, we received the call. We rechecked all our gear that had already been checked and checked again and moved to the airstrip. We were being taken to Turkey by two USAF long-distance, high-altitude surveillance planes. In the next phase we would load onto the stealth aircraft and be dropped close to Oral. We would need compact oxygen tanks, full jump gear, and would be using the latest in parachutes.

The chutes were also invisible and able to handle tremendous stress while maintaining excellent manoeuverability. As we settled into the transport, we reviewed all the weapons we were carrying and talked about what we were about to do for the planet. We had plenty of time as that flight to Turkey was close to fourteen hours.

We talked and planned and then racked-out for a few hours so we would be fresh when we arrived. We all awoke almost simultaneously as the aircraft began to descend into Incirlik air base. The base is shared by the US and Turkish Air Forces and is only about 30 km inland from the Mediterranean Sea. It is home to the Turkish Air Force 10th Tanker Base Command and also the USAF 39th Air Base Wing.

Once on the ground, we taxied directly to the front of a hangar and were told to remain in place and prepare all our gear. It wasn't lost on any of us that this might be the last time we were ever on friendly soil!

I made a half-promise that if we DID get home, I would seriously consider leaving the service, permanently this time.

Chapter Fifty 4 – First, A Little SEAL Activity

We were then advised to hold until further notice. Apparently, there had been a change of plans and we were delayed. They further advised it could be up to two weeks. We would get three to four days notice thanks to our inside contact so that was great.

We knew we had some time to wait before we would be able to move to Oral and complete our mission. There are two things that SEALs are well known for: finishing our missions and blowing stuff up. Heck, underwater demolition is one of the areas on which we trained extensively, it's even got an acronym of its own, BUDS. Basic Underwater Demolition/SEAL.

It was not in the original plan but seeing how Ukraine was being devastated we wanted to help them send the message that they would not go quietly into the night. We knew that simply taking out their leader would not stop hostilities immediately, so we decided to help out a bit. We were aware that if we were caught, we could very well be the cause of another World War, but we could not stand by while innocent people were being killed.

Getting from Turkey to the port city of Mariupol was no small feat in itself but we managed to get that done thanks to some helpful Ukrainians. The Russians were supplying their troops and also moving equipment in via the port of Berdyansk, on the Sea of Azov.

They seemed to hold little regard for the Ukrainian fighters and were not concerned. We had been informed there were going to be a number of ships there in two days and hoped we had enough time to get in, do a little work and get out.

Luba had been working closely with Ukrainian special forces and had arranged for everything we needed. When we arrived, there was scuba equipment with rebreathers (almost no bubbles produced) as well as all the other equipment we had asked for. The supplies included a new version of RDX explosive. RDX is a derivative of TNT and on its own is very unstable.

It is too unstable to work with to trigger an underwater explosion, but this was an RDX variant that was much more stable. There were drawings of the ships that were now in the port, and we reviewed them closely.

None were nuclear powered, which made destroying them a little easier. The full fuel tanks on the ships could be triggered to explode which would cause maximum damage. This would not only cripple the ships and all the cargo on them but also prevent the massive stores of fuel from getting to the Russian tanks and personnel carriers.

We had to plan quickly and prepare the various charges including mapping out where each had to be placed. We completed all our prep work and when nightfall arrived, we began to move towards Berdyansk from Mariupol.

Soon the three of us were in the water, the charges securely held in bags strapped to our tanks. It was a strange feeling to know that if something went wrong while we were transporting these, we would be vaporized. There would not be so much as one trace remaining.

As I moved through the water towards "my" ship I felt a sense of calm that often came over me when I knew what I was doing was righteous and just. Certainly, there were Russian troops who did not want to be here but that didn't matter. They had already blown up a maternity hospital and there had been rumors that vacuum bombs were even being used.

Each of us knew that destroying the supplies on these ships would save many Ukrainian lives.

I swam easily, using the gps display on my mask to guide me through the dark waters. Mariupol is quite close to the Russian border and Berdyansk is only about 78 kilometres further down the coast of Ukraine. As I contemplated those distances my sense of calm began to dissipate with the knowledge of how close we were to the bear.

Almost out of nowhere, I was suddenly against the massive hull of the supply ship.

I began to work my way along the steel behemoth as my gps targeted the required location for me. Breathe in slowly, breathe out slowly, I repeated over and over in my head as I swam as steadily as possible. Finally, I was looking at a red dot on my visor that signified the ideal location.

I removed the straps and gingerly prepared the charges. There were three timed to go off seconds apart and placed in a triangular pattern. The first was a shaped charge designed to blow a massive hole up into the ship. The other two charges would be pulled up and then detonate inside the hull itself and that would be that. Each set of charges were interconnected in this manner so the only required setting was the first shaped charge. Everything after that first detonate command would be automatic.

There was some concern between us that this little side mission might jeopardize our main mission. When that was tabled, we all immediately agreed that Vladimir's own ego would mean he would still rendezvous with his new friend in Oral. Unlike Volodymyr Zelenskyy, Vlad chose to stay as far away from the actual fighting as he could.

Zelenskyy, the previously not too popular President of Ukraine, is quite the story. He was an actor and a comedian before becoming President. He won the Presidency in what could be considered a very Western way. He never did release a policy platform and stayed away from mainstream media.

During the four months when he was "campaigning" he used social media and you tube as his main method of communication. His personal campaigning was in the form of stand-up comedy routines with his Kvartal 95 comedy group.

He was sworn in on May 20, 2019, and up until Russia attacked his country his popularity was on a steady downhill trajectory. That trajectory completely reversed as he took the lead defending his country and people.

I supposed that the Russian leader is most likely a little jealous of Zelenskyy who is a full 25 years younger and clearly, twice the man. I suspected that Vlad was also envious that Zelenskyy is married to a stunning former screenwriter who is the same age as her husband. Olena Zelenska has the fine features of a fashion model coupled with an intellect that allows her to be successful in many areas.

After about thirty minutes of swimming through the port I met back up with Sonny and Travis on the shore. We were being transported back to a spot outside Mariupol and on the way, we watched the first ship explode on the horizon. It lit up the night sky, so we knew that maximum damage had been inflicted. The other two went up just as well. Our Ukrainian guides all cheered wildly when the explosions happened.

Now that we were done, we needed to get back to Turkey. It was a long way to go only to backtrack to return to Kazakhstan, but it was deemed the safest approach.

Chapter Fifty 5 – Go Time

Two days after we returned to Turkey we were directed into the hangar where our "transport" was fueled and ready to go. As we walked through the door, I was struck by the 30th century appearance of the craft. It looked like a cross between an airliner, a fighter jet, and a spaceship. We tossed our gear in through the door and were given a quick tour.

We would be dropping out of the Bombay doors but would be on more of an ejection platform that had been adapted for humans. The plane would be dipping as we jumped, and the platforms would launch each of us safely away. The Captain advised that this had never been attempted before but they did trial ones with bodyweight dummies, and everything worked well. THAT was a real confidence builder.

Oh well, the jump itself was the most difficult and dangerous part. A HALO jump from this altitude had a lot of moving parts and even the smallest mistake could mean the end. I was confident that we had been trained to be perfect and felt reasonably good about it as did the boys.

We had GPS coordinates dialed into our helmets and directional guidance would be provided on our visors. It was sort of like a heads-up display on the windshield of your car. Pretty cool stuff really.

There were both visual and audio warnings ten seconds and five seconds prior to pulling your chute. At the ten second warning you would transition to a belly down position to grab as much air as possible and slow your descent. That gave a full ten seconds to scrub off enough speed so the chute would not rip to shreds when deployed.

Although there was an option to carry an auxiliary chute, in the best-case scenario that would slow you enough so you would likely only break arms and legs. You would then be a sitting duck so all three of us eschewed the aux-chute and opted for additional ammo. We had each made many tactical jumps and SEALs are the kings of the HALO jump, so we were confident. We were ready, as always.

The key was to plummet towards the earth at top speed as long as absolutely possible to minimize the chances of leaving a radar signature. These new chutes were not a guarantee of invisibility. We would leave Incirlik and climb very quickly to over 50,000 feet, up into the Stratosphere of the earth.

The good thing about the area where we were planning to land is that it is predominantly agricultural. Sitting along the Ural river, and with farming as its main industry, it was a little Midwest-ish. I hoped the familiar topography would be somewhat comforting.

We strapped into our seats and prepared for the ride of a lifetime, according to our pilot. We heard the powerful turbojets quickly ramp up to full power as he released the brakes. Seconds later we were literally rocketing down the runway until the plane began its rapid ascent. As it did a great many thoughts raced through my mind.

Our helmets were on, and we were plugged into plane oxygen so there was no discussion. Besides, I knew Sonny and Travis were like me. The less said the better.

The average flight time on a commercial airline from Turkey to Oral is about four hours. They fly at roughly 525 mph. The aircraft we were in flew at close to three times that speed or more, similar to the F-22 Raptor. We asked the speed and Captain said that was classified.

We all chuckled as we said, almost at the same time, no problem, we can do the math. He smiled and said we should expect to be over target in just a little more than an hour. WOW! That is indeed some kind of speed, and we were all immediately excited about the ride.

Speed was good as the Russians still had the fastest fighter on the planet, the MiG-25 Foxbat.

It could cruise at Mach 2.8 and had a top speed of Mach 3.2. Just so you know, Mach 2.8 is more than 2,100 miles per hour. To put that in perspective that means it travels more than 35 miles each MINUTE! Since we have nothing to match that speed, that we are aware of, the US has invested heavily in stealth concepts.

In what seemed like no time at all, we got the buzzer that we were fifteen mics out, so we unbuckled and got all our gear ready. Our weapons and tactical bags sat flat underneath our chutes. We each double checked the heads-up display in our helmets and coms and singled to each other we were ready. Each one of us went to our ejection platform and then we heard the next buzzer. One minute to drop zone.

We looked at each other with a thumbs up and saw the navigator do the same. The plane had already begun a hard descent and then the doors opened and out we went, one after another. It was like I imagined being shot out of a cannon might feel like. The helmets and coms kept everything quiet, and it was a little surreal travelling at almost 180 mph with only the sound of the oxygen tank providing its life sustaining vapor.

There would be no communication in the air, just a 100% focus on our displays and where we needed to guide ourselves. We each pointed ourselves towards terra firma like rocketmen, as we streaked silently through the night sky.

Even from 35,000 feet up, the plunge wouldn't take long. It would be about 3 minutes to reach the altitude at which we would need to deploy our chutes.

Then I heard and saw my ten second warning. I had adjusted my trajectory just prior and was comfortable with where I was. I oriented my belly towards the earth and felt my speed slowing. I double checked my display, heard the five second warning, and moved my hand to my chute release. At this point it would be just another night sky-dive, provided nothing went wrong.

I pulled my chute and looked around. All our chutes had deployed smoothly and now we were driving them towards the coordinates given.

We landed in a field that seemed to be in the middle of nowhere and quickly gathered our chutes into a pile.

We heard noise and then saw a very quick flash of a light as a vehicle rolled toward us. Sonny and Travis took up positions on each of my flanks, weapons drawn just in case.

The truck rolled up and I was greeted by our contact. I waved to the boys that everything was okay.

There was only the driver, and he was clearly unarmed. We quickly threw everything into the back of the truck. With no lights anywhere, including no headlights, we bounced through the field.

Our contact said only, "You will be safe here," as we drove into a large barn with a faint red light glowing. Another person guided us over to a hidden trap door in the floor with stairs that led down to what was evidently a well-equipped bomb shelter, or something similar. Before leaving he said that an American would arrive soon to pick us up.

It was about an hour later, when we heard the trap door open and an American voice saying we needed to get moving. We loaded our gear into the trunk of the vehicle and when we got into the car, he handed us each papers. Although we were not crossing any borders, he advised that all travellers in Kazakhstan carried their papers wherever they went, especially now.

Turned out he was CIA and had been embedded in Kazakhstan for more than three years. He had a network of contacts and had been keeping a close eye on Russia from right next door.

As we drove, he explained it would take us about three hours to arrive in Oral. He said we were welcome to sleep if we wished. In typical SEAL fashion, we each took turns while the other maintained vigilance. We each grabbed a few Z's but when there was about an hour left in our drive, we were all on high alert. Harold said that we would be staying in a house a block away from where Vlad was.

He described the layout of the house including access and egress points. At the end he added that there was a series of tunnels which we could use to get in and out, but we had to know the other routes in case they were compromised. The best news was that the guards and sentries were all around the outside of the house and next door, but the leader wanted his privacy. Once he and the girl were in the house, they were never disturbed for at least 36 – 48 hours. That just showed the cockiness he has always displayed, not thinking for even a second that anyone could get this close.

He said the information was classified but the CIA had actually built the tunnels during construction of the house and a couple around it. The Russian maniac had no idea he was spending all his time there almost fully exposed. We finally rolled into the compound where we would be basing our operations.

We got safely inside and began to review maps. The house we were in was between two universities, close to the Chagan River.

The CIA had a contact at the West Kazakhstan State University that seemed to always know what was happening everywhere. Harold relied on him extensively.

While the majority of the Kazakhs were supportive of Russia, there were many in academia who were against any relationship with them subsequent to the breakup of the USSR. Harold's "guy" was one of those dissenters.

Chapter Fifty 6 – Saving Ukraine

About two hours after settling in we were advised that it was time to move. Harold took us to the tunnel entrance after we discussed the layout of the house one final time. This was it. We were getting a chance to profoundly change the course of history and save a country, perhaps even the world, from a madman. The responsibility was not lost on any of us.

Each of us was ready for multiple scenarios, including having to blast our way out of there. We also knew that if we did have to exit that way this would immediately become a suicide mission after all. None of us wanted that. We wanted to get in, do our job and get out. Hopefully, without disturbing a soul. We would need as much time as possible to get to Aktau and begin our escape.

Aktau is a city that sits next to the Caspian Sea. There is a large marina to be built there to cater to the growing yacht and superyacht industry in the region. Currently, there is a smaller but still packed existing marina. Some of the ridiculously rich Russian oligarchs can be found yachting on the Caspian, typically in one of their smaller yachts.

IF we could get that far, we were going to be able to hide in a yacht and get to Azerbaijan. That country was nowhere near as friendly towards Russia as Kazakhstan is.

Since the breakup of the Soviet Union, Azerbaijan established diplomatic relations with the USA. Their main goal is European energy security but there are two other pillars of the arrangement, expand trade and investment, and combat terrorism.

Unbeknownst to Vladimir, there were super-wealthy oligarchs who were not supporters of what he was doing, especially behind the scenes. The CIA had apparently enlisted the help of one of these people. It was a tenuous plan, held together mostly with the threads of hope, but at least it was a plan. A chance to save the planet. An opportunity to rescue the brave Ukraine.

Our minds now needed to be on the task at hand. We could worry about escape later. I know that each of us was completely focused as we moved on all fours through the tunnel. The timing should be good. It was now about three hours after the dinner hour, so it was likely the two were in the midst of some sort of carnal pleasure. It didn't matter what they were doing as, even if there were guards stationed inside the house, they would be no match for us.

I briefly reached into my pocket to check for my trusty garotte. We each had multiple knives strapped to our bodies as well.

A tough leather scabbard holding a knife on your forearm also acted as a great defense, depending upon what we ran up against. Soon the three of us were at the tunnel exit which terminated inside a bedroom closet.

With the utmost stealth, we slowly emerged, knives in hand and ready for anything. Thankfully, the door was ajar, so we were able to look into the hallway and confirm there were no guards nearby. Hopefully, there were none inside the house at all, as we were told, but you could never really trust intelligence I've found.

Sonny moved slowly out into the hallway and then waved us forward.

We were now outside the door and when we heard the shower running, we made our move. We went silently into the room and were shocked when we all saw the girl on the bed. I moved quickly to silence her but there was no need, she simply smiled and pointed to the bathroom. I had no idea what her deal was but would find out later the CIA had successfully gotten an agent sleeping with the Russian leader.

It was far easier than expected apparently, and it was accomplished when that photo showed of him riding shirtless on a horse. After that, it was all narcissism that got her embedded. I readied my garotte and stood next to the bathroom door for what seemed like an eternity. Sonny and Travis were on either side of the door just in case but there would be no need.

Vlad strode proudly out of the bathroom with his typical air of invincibility only to discover that had evaporated. I moved quickly and twisted the loop over his head as I pulled hard enough to silence him. He made no noise as I pulled him backwards off his feet and held his life in my hands. He gurgled and kicked as he moved closer to his death.

I was caught a little by surprise when the girl got up from the bed, casually walked toward him, and kicked him hard in the groin. "Die you bastard, die," was all she said.

Once the life had been squeezed out of him the four of us quickly returned to the tunnel and made our way back.

We had no idea we would be having to drag another person out with us. As we prepared to leave, she highlighted that now we could travel as if we were two couples. The fact she was Kazakh might also help.

I didn't like relying on anyone but a brother SEAL, but this was now our best option. We left the bulk of our weapons behind as we changed into local clothing. As we dressed, we smiled at each other as we noted where all the knives were positioned on each of us. I suppose unarmed was more a state of mind than anything.

Chapter Fifty 7 – Escape Certain Death

In minutes we were in a vehicle and headed towards the coast. We were already motoring pretty well as we really needed to escape the area before he was discovered. Aktau was not THAT far South of the Russian border so we were by no means feeling safe. That being said, we still had almost 1,400 kilometres to cover, without drawing attention to ourselves.

Gratefully, the bulk of those km's were on a significant highway in the area. It took less than 17 hours with minimal stopping and moving with the flow of traffic. We never discussed it, but I knew all three of us were concerned about putting our lives into the hands of an oligarch. The girl had told us that she had made a big deal of wanting to spend three full days with Max so, if all went well, we should be on the yacht before the alarms went off.

Getting to Azerbaijan was certainly no guarantee of freedom but it did get us that much closer to Turkey. Once we got back to Incirlik air base we would be immediately flown home.

We drove to the marina and spotted the yacht on which we were to hopefully sail towards our freedom. We drove directly to a stall and parked and then moved down the marina to a large, but not super large yacht. I figured it to be about 30 metres in length, about 90 feet. Big certainly, but not oligarch big.

As we boarded and were ushered inside, I did notice that it was very well equipped and clearly not a bargain basement boat. As we were shown to our rooms, I noticed some photos of a different yacht, much larger, that looked a bit like a destroyer. I would find out that one, the Aliyona, was over 100 metres in length and worth in excess of 500 million dollars. I supposed money could buy happiness, if that sort of possession made you happy.

We settled in and kept to our rooms. We were specifically not to meet or speak with anyone, for our safety and theirs. We relaxed as best we could as we motored across the Caspian towards Azerbaijan. After what felt like a days long trip, we pulled into a landing close to Baku, on a small peninsula that jutted out into the Caspian.

We now had to cross through Azerbaijan and Armenia to get to Turkey. Fortunately, we did not have to go through Georgia, as that country was still very Russian-friendly. During that trip we were notified that Vladimir had been discovered dead and they were looking for the girl. They assumed she had somehow killed him and were fixated on that. That fact might be what helps us get out. It might also help when the US begins talks with whomever takes over Russia.

Our agent had already cut her hair, changed the color, added some glasses, and changed her look in other ways.

She matched the papers she had so everything was on track. We were driving in an older Renault Sandero, the most popular car in that country, so we blended in well. It was like a small SUV but was really a car. They were cheap and plentiful so offered great cover for us, although not the most comfortable of rides.

It was going to be a long trip, and we all would have preferred to fly, but this was the safest way for us to move about. We settled in for a trip of over 2,000 km. We kept to ourselves stopping only to gas up and for the odd bio break. There wasn't a lot of talking going on as the three of us kept a close eye on everything around us. Our CIA lady didn't contribute much but I supposed she had done her job. One which I could never have accomplished. No, I did what I was best at and that was all I needed to know.

As we pulled into Incirlik I made a small prayer of thanks in my mind. I knew that a higher power MUST have guided us. I returned to the present in my mind as our plane lifted off from Incirlik to return us to the safety of US soil. I wasn't sure I would drop down and kiss the tarmac, but it felt like a real possibility as the gravity of what we had done began to sink in.

We were told we could relax as we were all in safe hands now and would be flying direct to NAB Coronado. Home sweet home to be sure.

I looked through the cockpit and out the front of the aircraft where you could see the curvature of the earth and the horizon beyond that. As the sun began to set the sky was lit up with all shades of red, orange, and yellow until there was finally just a corona-like glow above the horizon.

It truly was a beautiful thing to see, especially for us right at this moment. I was surprised when I awoke from a deep sleep as the plane touched down at Coronado. There were two black suburbans waiting at the doors as we taxied to a stop. The three of us were directed to one and the CIA agent to the other. That would be the last we would see of her, with little more than a nod of her head she was gone.

We were driven directly to one of the smaller, private ready rooms on the base where we were greeted by SECNAV.

Tom shook each of our hands and thanked us for our service. He went on to tell us that things were already happening. There were still plans for a massive state funeral, but troops were already moving out of Ukraine. It turned out the number two man in Russia, Dmitry Medvedev, was not as supportive of his President-for-life's goals as it had appeared. He is Chairman of the Security Council of Russia, and he apparently believes in democracy.

Conveniently, he also has some relatives who are Ukrainian. His only daughter married a Ukrainian man. I was certain this knowledge factored into the plan we had just executed. At any rate, it was done. The three of us had set things in motion to restore the world order and it felt pretty damn good.

We had to remain on base for another day to further debrief but Tom thanked us again and said to have a nice retirement. That was that.

Chapter Fifty 8 - Home At Last

That was a mission I was super happy to be over. It was ugly and there were so many innocent people at risk. Thankfully, we had been able to stop the attack, but those scars would last a lifetime. I tried to clear my head of all of it as I lounged on my roof deck and sipped on some sun tea.

It was another in a seemingly endless line of sunny, warm days, and I was soaking it all in. Kathy and Angela had already been in touch, but it was too soon for me to attend any public gatherings. I found that I really needed time to get out of my head and simply be fully present in California.

My shrink helped me understand that during the first week or two after a mission I was in the most danger of being triggered and doing something from which I may not be able to walk away. It goes back to the whole PTSD thing that so many of our veterans suffer from. The average person just cannot understand what it is like to be in war of any type and then try to return to a normal life. You spend so much time living on a hair trigger that some just never come back.

I did not want to be one of those people. I wanted to be gone whenever I decided, and I wanted it to be on my terms. It wasn't that I enjoyed the killing or anything sick like that.

I enjoyed making a difference in the world. I liked to help other women and girls be strong, make their own way, and live happily and safely. I was beginning to decide what I might like to do once I was done serving but had plenty of time to figure that out. For now, I just needed to relax.

I took a couple of weeks of getting back to training and taking nice long runs up and down the beach. I thought about little, did less, and just enjoyed the lifestyle to which I really wanted to become accustomed. I wasn't completely certain I could actually retire although, thanks to Jonathon's investing tips, I certainly had more cash than I needed so it wasn't about money.

At the same time, it seemed that I was losing my zeal for surfing. I still loved being out on the water but the thrill of dominating those waves seemed to have diminished. It was strange to feel like that. I had enjoyed surfing so much and, with Dukie's help, had really gotten good. I took my board out a couple of times and had some decent rides but that was about it. Decent rides. I felt like something had been taken from me, so I began to look for a replacement.

That replacement would be a return to something I did when I was much younger, sailing. I had loved sailing. The challenge of reading the winds, planning, and reacting to get the most from your boat, was really enjoyable. There is a lot more to sailing than the average Joe is aware.

I decided that when the dust settled, I would acquire the right type of boat. I knew I wanted something 35-45 feet so that I could comfortably live aboard if I chose to.

A catamaran, with the right power equipment and power sail rigging, could be handled by one person if it was properly equipped. It's not like I'd go around the world by myself or anything, but I did not want to be forced to depend on others.

I would also explore some high-end monohulls like the Beneteau Oceanis series. Again, with the right power assist and sail package you could enjoy it alone or with just one other guest.

I began to think I might like one other guest. I just had no idea who that might be. I was also quite comfortable being alone. It wasn't like I NEEDED anyone. As long as I had all my friends relatively close, I knew I could be happy. That was when it hit me.

I knew I wanted to be close to all my friends and I DID have that great house, thanks to my aunt but I still wanted something different. I quickly decided on that something different. Where could I live on a boat, enjoy myself but not be isolated from my friends?

Chapter Fifty 9 – Avalon

Off the coast of California, on Santa Catalina island, is Avalon. It had everything and it was a safe, ocean front community where one could easily live on a boat for as long as you wished. Every time I head that song Avalon, when Bryan Ferry was still with Roxy Music, I thought of this place. Peaceful, serene, and still California. I put a reminder to myself to download that album and already envisioned myself laying out on my boat with that playing in the background.

Avalon was a microcosm of the California beach lifestyle. An idyllic little place nestled in the hills surrounding Catalina Bay. It was on the Southern end of the island and offered tremendous diving and was excellent for sailing. I had no idea where I might sail to or if I would simply sail around the area, but I knew what I wanted. I began searching for the perfect boat.

While there were many monohulls to choose from, I had decided a catamaran made more sense. They were simpler to sail for one or two people and provided a large, open, main deck salon where there was plenty of room to relax and watch the sun set or rise. I engaged a yacht broker that Jonathon was familiar with, and my search began.

It didn't take long for them to find me the right boat. It is a Bali 4.3. A 43-foot catamaran that was ideal for what I wanted.

At 43 feet it was quite easy to handle, and it had tons of automation as well. The broker showed me one equipped the same as this one and it seemed pretty ideal. The center cockpit, single helm design enabled the positioning of all necessary controls close at hand. One person could sail this craft it was so completely automated. I suppose that was what a ¾ million-dollar sailboat SHOULD be like!

I was sold the minute we walked on board. It had a large main level seating and dining area that could be either closed or open to the weather. There were three bedrooms, staterooms in sailor lingo I suppose, and two powerful diesel engines in case there was no wind. It was designed so that three to four couples or up to eight people could sail across the ocean quite comfortably.

It was not super extravagant, but it was definitely a lot more than I had ever seen, except for the yacht that ferried us across the Caspian. That already seemed like a lifetime ago. I knew I had done the right thing for my country, the world and especially Ukraine but it still weighed on me as a person.

The boat was currently "living" in the South Pacific and when the broker asked if I wanted to sail her home, I politely declined. As an inexperienced sailor I had no desire to pilot a craft across the largest and deepest of our five oceans.

Nope, I said I would leave it to him to make those arrangements. In the meanwhile, I would lock up a boat slip on Catalina Island and then simply wait for delivery.

I had the specs for the boat in hand when I went to tour the marina. It would be no challenge at all to live on her for ½ the year.

Residential appliances including fridge, stove, dishwasher, and washer dryer would make it easy. There was even a trash compacter. As I expected, Jonathon "knew a guy" who had close ties to the marina there, so he put in a call before I went over.

The broker had advised that I would require shore power designed for a much larger yacht because of the equipment on her. Jonathon's guy turned out to be very helpful and I ended up located at the far side of the marina on the outside row. It had a beautiful view of the Pacific and the spectacular sunrises. Due to the orientation of the valley that Avalon was carved into, and the marina orientation, you didn't get much sunset view.

The good news was all you had to do to catch beautiful sunsets was sail around the island to Starlight Beach and drop anchor. Within two months my new home away from home was being delivered and maneuvered into my slip. It somehow looked even more impressive now, simply because it was mine. I couldn't wait to have everyone over.

I got settled in and fully provisioned and I decided I was ready. I knew exactly who I wanted for my first boat slumber party. Kathy and Jonathon, Luke and Angela, Colin and there was no way Norie would not be invited. I couldn't wait to kick things off and I was on the phone to everyone as soon as I returned to the mainland.

They were all pretty pumped about the whole thing. Why not? Everyone loved Catalina.

Chapter 60 – My Second Home

The time had finally arrived. I walked over to the ferry to meet Jonathon and Kathy. Everyone else was arriving the next day. The three of us strolled along the waterfront to my slip and got on board. I had a splendid view of the former Casino that was now an arts hub, and the dive park was right off the end of that.

I gave them the cooks tour and they both seemed impressed and happy for me. I was happy for me too! I had busted my butt to get this, although it was Jonathon's investment tips that got me the cash to take this plunge. I thanked him for convincing me to let him build my portfolio. I said that without him none of this would have been possible.

We had a great evening, did a little swimming after dinner, and planned to go fishing in the morning. The tender I had was large enough that I could leave the cat moored until the rest of my guests arrived. When they did, I decided we would sail around to Starlight and moor there so we could all watch the sunset up close as our feet dangled over the edge of my home on the water.

I remembered Jonathon's special margarita machine he had built and had a few tricks up my sleeve too in my outdoor bar. When he saw my cocktail Keurig, I could tell he was impressed.

It worked like the coffee machines did. It had various pods with different drink mixes and a container for liquor and a container for water. It really was pretty cool.

We just relaxed and hung out and enjoyed the evening. We all crashed relatively early so we could save ourselves for the next evening.

We were all up on deck and Jonathon was especially eager to get fishing. His buddy there gave him the GPS coordinates for a great fishing spot. In no time, we were off into the ocean. His pal had said we were most likely to catch Calico bass in that location and it's a great sport fish. Unfortunately, it is not recommended for eating, like many slow growing fish. That didn't bother us as I had plenty of food ready to go back on the boat.

We had an excellent few hours, lounging in the sun and dangling our lines in the water. Jonathon hooked a pretty good-sized Calico, but Kathy and I came up empty. Oh well, it was close to time to head back so we weren't concerned at all. We motored back, tied off and that took a leisurely stroll over to the ferry dock. The gang were all on the same sailing so that made it easy.

Today was actually Luke's birthday as well, so he got a free ticket. Not like they would ever care about saving 76 bucks, but whatever. We all had a good laugh about it when we stopped at the Bluewater Grill for drinks and a snack. It was one of the newer restaurants in Avalon and was perched over the sand and water. Fortunately, I had booked ahead so we were able to get a great table on the deck.

Sitting there you had relaxing views including the bay, the Avalon pier and even the endless rows of moored boats. I had already discovered their cilantro-lime mussels, so we had a few plates of those. We ended up not leaving until about 2:30 or so but that was fine. We walked back to my boat and after giving everyone a tour and showing them their rooms, I said we had better get underway.

The girls wasted no time getting into their bikinis and heading to the rope sun deck at the bow, suspended between the two hulls, it was like one giant, comfy hammock. Sadly, there was no wind today, so I was motoring again but that was fine. It made the ride up front very nice indeed. The odd sea splash of cooling mist coming up from below as the sun baked you on the top.

While you could actually see the sunset from my mooring it was cut off by the protruding peninsula of the island itself.

It looked rather good I had noticed but I really wanted the whole visual, so I had decided on Emerald Bay and followed the shoreline around to that point.

We dropped anchor in a nice, secluded spot and I turned Jonathon loose on the grill. Soon, we were all enjoying some char broiled oysters, New Orleans style, along with lots of other tasty foods. In addition to my cocktail maker, I had also stocked up with significant amounts of wine as that seemed to be the beverage of choice for this group.

As we all sat there and watched the brilliant blaze of the sun sinking slowly into the serene Pacific ocean, I thought there was absolutely no place I would rather be. I was in a beautiful spot, very South Pacific like, with my closest friends and not a care in the world.

In the far reaches of my mind I was already wondering how long care-free might actually last for me!

Other books in this series by C.C.Chamberlane
Abbadon
Samaela
Megan Hernandez – The First Female Navy SEAL

Don't miss out!

Visit the website below and you can sign up to receive emails whenever C. C. Chamberlane publishes a new book. There's no charge and no obligation.

https://books2read.com/r/B-A-JWSR-YIUWB

BOOKS 2 READ

Connecting independent readers to independent writers.

Also by C. C. Chamberlane

Megan Hernandez
Samaela
The First Female Navy SEAL
Saving Ukraine

Standalone
Abbadon

About the Author

C.C.Chamberlane has been a novelist for a few years now. His first series of books include; ABBADON, SAMAELA, the First Female Navy SEAL and Saving Ukraine.

These stories focus on Megan Hernandez and her power and commitment to do good in the world.

www.ingramcontent.com/pod-product-compliance
Lightning Source LLC
Chambersburg PA
CBHW031339020726
47499CB00005B/1336